Across the East River Bridge

Printed in the United States of America

Originally published in 2012 by Loose Id

Second Edition, 2015

Cover & Book Design by Kate McMurray

ISBN 978-0-9970328-1-9

Echo Hill Books
www.katemcmurray.com/echohill

Across the East River Bridge

Kate McMurray

Also by Kate McMurray

In Hot Pursuit
The Boy Next Door
Blind Items
Out in the Field
Four Corners
Show and Tell
The Stars that Tremble
The Silence of the Stars
When the Planets Align
Such a Dance
Ten Days in August

The Rainbow League Series
The Windup
Thrown a Curve
The Long Slide Home

Across the East River Bridge

When historian Christopher Finnegan walks into a new museum in Brooklyn, he's chagrined to learn its curator is his old academic rival, Troy Rafferty. Worse, Troy is convinced the museum is haunted and wants Finn's help learning more about the ghosts. Finn and Troy have never gotten along and Finn wants to run screaming, but then Troy offers him an intriguing proposal: Troy will help Finn with a research project for his overbearing boss if Finn will help Troy solve a mystery involving two men who died in the building under mysterious circumstances in 1878.

Finn and Troy piece together the two men's lives—and the quiet romance that grew between them—through diaries, newspaper clippings, and police reports. They're both soon convinced the men were murdered. They're also convinced the ghosts are real—even Finn witnesses paranormal phenomena he can't deny—and that they're capable of affecting thoughts, feelings, and actions. When Finn and Troy start falling for each other despite years of animosity, Finn worries he's being manipulated by the ghosts to stay with Troy and solve the case. Troy is convinced the love between them is real, but he'll need to figure out how to get rid of the ghosts in order to prove it.

Chapter 1

The squeal of the subway train's brakes as it pulled into the station intensified Finn's headache, making the pain reverberate through his head. The bumpy ride once he got on the train didn't help much either. This was but one of many reasons he rarely left Manhattan.

Finn closed his eyes and leaned back in his seat. He mentally ran through his to-do list for the day and felt exhausted just thinking about it. The vibrations from the train intensified his headache, making it hard to think. He needed to get this little side trip over with. Then he just had a few more hours to work before he could go to sleep.

It was because of Loretta Kitteredge that he found himself in Brooklyn a short time later. She had dispatched him on a fact-finding mission. Loretta was in the midst of writing the definitive biography of Victoria Woodhull, the first woman to run for president, and she was looking for some dirt. Rumor had it that Woodhull had lived briefly at the Brill House, a five-story brownstone in Brooklyn Heights, so Finn was on this wild-goose chase to find information he didn't think would be there. The Brill House was a recent acquisition of the Kings County Historical Society, which had converted the building into a museum showcasing what life was like in Brooklyn in the 1870s. Finn had scored an appointment with the curator.

Or that's what he thought when he went into the building. Instead, he was greeted in the lobby by Troy Rafferty, of all people. As if the day couldn't get any worse.

"What the hell are you doing here?" Finn asked, letting

his gaze travel over Troy's infuriatingly handsome face. He rubbed his temples gently, trying to get the ache to ease.

Their gazes met briefly. Troy was still hot in a Clark Kent kind of way, his broad chest hidden under an eggplant-colored button-down shirt and matching tie, dark-rimmed glasses sitting on his nose, dark hair neatly combed. Finn silently lamented that his enemies had to come in such attractive packages.

Troy laughed. "It is lovely to see you again too. As it happens, I curate this house."

Finn knew Troy worked for the KCHS, but this promotion was news to him. "You're kidding, right? I made an appointment with a woman named Genevieve."

Troy's grin was unnerving. "Genevieve is my assistant. She has been doing the tours lately, but when I saw that she'd made an appointment with one Christopher Finnegan, I decided I had to follow up myself." He straightened the cuffs on his shirt, drawing attention to his big hands. "How are you, Finn?"

"Oh, just dandy. If I didn't know better, I'd say you were stalking me."

"You give me too much credit." Troy motioned for Finn to follow him into an office off the lobby. The room looked like the relic of the past that it was—with ornate wallpaper, thick curtains, and a severe-looking man frowning in painting on the wall—if you overlooked the brand-new laptop sitting on the intricately carved desk. There was a lot of clutter too; Troy had never been terribly organized. He clucked his tongue. "Or maybe you're right. Obviously, I knew that you would one day be researching a project on nineteenth-century Brooklyn, so I quit my job at NYU to take a low-paying assistant curator job at the Kings County

Historical Society in the hopes that one day I'd curate the museum in an old house the KCHS just acquired three months ago, knowing you'd want an appointment."

"Shut up," was the best witty rejoinder Finn could come up with. He blamed the headache.

Troy picked up a file folder from his desk and extracted a few sheets of paper. "This is the fact sheet," he said, handing the paper to Finn. "That has all the same information as went into the press release we put out when we announced the museum's opening, plus a few other facts that I thought the public might find interesting. The other two pages are a brief history of the building that I wrote up for the Historical Society. Was there something in particular you're looking for?"

"My boss is researching Victoria Woodhull."

Troy pursed his lips. "Are you sure *you're* not stalking *me?*" He shook his head. "Right time period but otherwise wrong tree. Woodhull never lived in Brooklyn, as far as I know."

Finn already suspected that this trip out to Brooklyn was a dead end. Woodhull had spent most of her years in New York in the same house in East Village, and the date Finn had been given for Woodhull's supposed residence at the Brill House conflicted with the date she'd left for England to start over after she'd been ruined. Still, Loretta had insisted he check it out. Plus he didn't want to waste the trip. "She spent time in the area. She gave speeches in Brooklyn, for sure one at the Brooklyn Academy of Music, and it's pretty well known that she befriended Theodore Tilton. He lived a few blocks from here, right? As did Henry Ward Beecher."

Troy appeared to consider this. "I've spent the better part of the last two months poring over almost everything ever written about this house. If Victoria Woodhull had ever been here, I'd have run across her name. I'm pretty sure I haven't yet." He shrugged. "You want the tour anyway?"

Finn *had* come all the way into Brooklyn. "Sure, what the hell?"

Troy grabbed a small notebook from his desk. "Let's go."

He led Finn down the hall. Finn took a moment to check Troy out again; looking at him certainly stirred something in Finn. Troy had always been classically handsome, but whether it was his good looks or their long history together that got Finn's blood pumping, it was hard to say. Probably a little of both. Finn found that frustrating; this would be so much easier if he could just get the information he needed and leave without having to think about all of this.

"We're setting up exhibits on the first, second, and third floors. The fourth floor is the library, and the fifth floor is mostly storage. The third floor has a portrait gallery of famous residents of Victorian Brooklyn and a gallery of mediocre landscapes by Brooklyn artists, mostly the cast-offs of the main KCHS museum. Do you care about those?"

"Not especially."

Troy nodded and continued walking toward a stairwell. He mounted the first step and said, "I want to add a photography gallery, but I'm still sorting through several boxes of prints from the KCHS archive. I'll keep an eye out for Ms. Woodhull."

"Thanks. What's on the second floor?"

Troy smiled. "This is the real highlight of the museum, as far as I'm concerned. We've recreated what a building like this would have looked like in the 1870s. A lot of this furniture was in storage at the KCHS or other museums in the city, waiting for a home. Some of the pieces are really extraordinary."

When they got to the second floor, Finn followed Troy into what looked like a bedroom. There was a grandiose four-poster bed off to the side with heavy green damask draped all around it. The bed was made of oak, Finn guessed, as was the ornate chest of drawers on the other side of the room.

"The building was originally constructed in 1868," Troy said, flipping through pages in his notebook. "It was intended to be a single-family residence according to the plan, but from very early on, before 1872 at least, the owner rented out rooms on the upper floors. My guess is he needed the income from the boarders. At any rate, this was the master bedroom. It's been many other things over the years, too, and this whole building was converted into apartments in the sixties, but this is our best guess for how the room would have looked when the first owner lived here. We had some floor plans and even a fuzzy photograph."

Finn wondered if he should be taking notes. "You've had to do a lot of work on this room."

"Yeah, in its last incarnation, this was a studio apartment with a kitchen and everything. We took out the kitchen. It's been kind of fun, watching this house devolve into its original form. Like backward time-lapse photography." Troy walked over to the bed and ran a finger up one of the posts. "The house is said to be haunted too."

"Oh, please."

"I've seen enough weird stuff that I can't stay completely skeptical, let's just say. There have been a number of documented ghostly occurrences here. A woman who lived here briefly in the forties kept a journal detailing her encounters with the spirits. Most of it's classic haunted-house stuff. Strange noises, cold blasts of air, doors suddenly slamming shut. Interestingly, almost every account of paranormal activity here indicates that the ghosts are two men."

"Okay." Finn had run into many ghost stories over the years he'd been working as a researcher and thought most of the stories were pure nonsense. He humored Troy, though, who seemed to be enjoying himself. "Do you know anything about who the ghosts might be?"

"No one has ever specified, but I have a guess." Troy's eyes practically sparkled with excitement.

"Did the previous owners know?"

"No, but I don't think they bothered to find out."

Troy enjoyed drawing things like this out, Finn knew. He held out a hand and motioned for Troy to keep talking. "What's your guess?"

"The first owner of this house was Theodore Cummings Brill. He was the youngest son of a large and moderately wealthy family. He and another man, George Washington Cutler, were found dead in this very bedroom in 1878."

A shiver went up Finn's spine. Someone had died in the room in which he was standing. "So that's who you think is haunting this house?"

"Yes. The facts fit, given when the sightings started." Troy walked closer to Finn. "I'm working on digging up causes of death. There was a story in the *Times*, but it was vague, saying only that the circumstances of their deaths were unusual. I've been piecing together other evidence, though."

"And you have a theory. You always have a theory."

"Suicide. Possibly murder-suicide, but I'm pretty sure they both took their own lives. Because they were gay."

Finn rolled his eyes. "You always think everyone was gay. You bought that horseshit about Lincoln being gay. Sometimes there's a simpler and much less biased explanation. What makes you think murder-suicide?"

"I can't remember offhand. Something I read, a contemporary account of the crime, I think. It makes more sense than any other theory of the crime I've seen." Troy rocked on his heels. "Some of the flooring is original. If you squint, you can still see the blood stains in the wood paneling on the floor."

Finn shivered again. "Show me something else." He left the room.

Troy's shoes squeaked on the floor as he caught up to Finn. "The theory has merits." He led Finn across the hall to another room. It had an elaborate sofa and a couple of chairs, everything Rococo revival. It was not a style Finn especially liked, but he knew it was popular in the 1870s. The upholstery on all of the pieces was beautiful, almost like new, except for a chaise longue in the corner that looked faded and worn.

Finn bent to take a closer look at the scrollwork on the sofa. Troy said, "This is the parlor. The furniture is mostly from the 1850s, but we had everything reupholstered, save for the chaise, obviously. The upholstery on the other pieces had disintegrated, but, I don't know, I kind of like the old faded quality on the chaise. What do you think?"

"I agree. It looks kind of…soft and homey." Finn meant it. He bet that chaise would be an excellent place to take a nap. Of course, thinking about that made Finn think about beds, and he had a sudden flash of Troy, hovering over him, naked. *That* certainly got his blood pumping. He coughed, trying to keep his body's reaction to the memory at bay. He reminded himself that he didn't like Troy much.

"Both men were bachelors," Troy said. Finn was about to stop him and ask who Troy was talking about but realized Troy was still on the alleged ghosts. "They were both in their midthirties when they died, but neither had ever been married, which is telling, don't you think?"

"Not so unusual as an unmarried woman," Finn said, trying to focus on the furniture.

"Fair enough. By all accounts, they were also very close friends."

"But, I'm guessing, not so close that there was any speculation. And may I remind you that men sharing beds with no sexual motives was not so unusual in the nineteenth century?"

"I hadn't even gotten to the bed-sharing part. I want the record to show that *you* made that conclusion." Troy walked over to Finn. "Have you been sharing *your* bed with any men lately?"

"Like that's your business," Finn said, though the truth was he hadn't, not since he'd taken the job with Loretta. There hadn't been time.

Troy seemed nonplussed. "Anyway, I'm not the first one to make the gay conclusion, thank you very much. There was speculation about them in their own time. I found a mention of them in the diary of Thomas Fledgeling Longwood, who lived a few houses over. Prolific diarist, I assume you're familiar." He tugged on the cuffs of his shirt again. "Anyway, you can't tell me you're not a little intrigued."

"I'm researching Woodhull."

"Of course. But come on! Murder, intrigue, a couple of men more than just friends way back in the nineteenth century, when going outside without a hat on was a scandal? That doesn't pique your interest at all?"

"It's interesting," Finn said. "Not the ghost stuff—that's a bedtime story—but two men who died under mysterious circumstances? You've got my attention, okay? Are you happy? It might be fun to pursue, but I'm up to my armpits in work for my paying job, and I don't have time to investigate, least of all with you."

"You wound me, Finn." Troy pressed a hand to his chest. "Are you still so petty after all the years we've known each other?"

Finn couldn't decide if he wanted to stay and spar verbally with Troy—just like they had in the good old days, back when Troy had been working at the Butler Library at Columbia and Finn had been fumbling his way toward an undergraduate degree in history—or run screaming from the building. Finn thought back on the last time he'd seen Troy, which made him lean toward the latter.

"It's not pettiness," he said. "You and I…don't work well together. Besides, what are you even proposing? That we buddy cop our way through solving a one-hundred-and-forty-year-old mystery, just for kicks? Because I don't know about you, but I work for a living."

"When did you get that stick up your ass?" Troy produced a handkerchief from his pocket, which Finn found pretentious but so typical of Troy, and then pulled his glasses from his face and wiped them off. He glanced up, and Finn was suddenly faced with the fact that Troy's blue eyes were stunning when they weren't hidden behind those lenses. Troy slid the glasses back on his face. "I know you've never liked me much, but I don't remember you being quite this hostile."

There was, of course, a lot more to it than that. The whole reason Finn was working for Loretta Kitteredge to begin with was that she was the only one who would hire him after he first failed to finish his PhD and then failed to finish his compromise masters in library science. Troy Rafferty had played a starring role in his first failure. It was hard to look at him, no matter how attractive he was, and not remember that. Because the bottom line was that he was still angry about how everything had gone down, even after all the time that had passed, even after everything that had happened since he dropped out of the PhD program at NYU. "Can you do me the favor of letting me know if you find anything on Woodhull? Even some photographs would be great. You're going through those old prints anyway, right?"

"Sure. Anything for an old friend." Troy gave Finn an ostentatious bow.

Chapter 2

Troy retreated to his office after Finn left, still somewhat off balance from their encounter. It had been fun teasing Finn at first, but the whole nice act had gone from trying to be polite to deliberately goading Finn pretty quickly. He hated himself a little for it, but he also wanted so much to wipe that smug look off Finn's beautiful face.

He sighed and woke up his computer. He had an e-mail from the library indicating several books he'd requested had come in. He glanced at the clock and was trying to decide if it was too early to duck out when Genevieve, a jovial woman in her sixties, knocked on his door.

"How'd the tour go?"

"Fine." Troy waved his hand.

"Old school friend of yours, right?"

Troy nodded. "Well, *friend* is relative. But I've known him since college, yes."

"You look tired, Troy. You should go home. Peter and I can close up."

Troy thanked her, and when she left, he wrapped up what he'd been working on before Finn had traipsed in. He tried to put the man out of his mind as he left the building.

He took the subway to the central branch of the Brooklyn Public Library. He'd always felt some comfort there; he especially liked the ostentatious façade, with the huge columns and gold accents, which made the whole building look like some kind of ancient temple. He hummed to himself as he picked up the books he had on hold; just being in the library soothed him. Then he found himself wandering through the nonfiction stacks. Thinking of Finn, he found an old biography of Victoria Woodhull and added it to his stack.

While he was on the second floor, he decided to pop into the Brooklyn Room, and sure enough, there was his old friend Darnell sitting behind the information desk, his head bobbing slowly to whatever music was being pumped into his headphones. The room was otherwise empty.

Troy dropped his books on the desk to get Darnell's attention. Darnell smiled and pulled off his headphones. "Hey, Helen," he said.

Troy smiled, trying not to react to hearing the nickname. "Hey. Are you still working on that Victorian Brooklyn project?"

"Nah. The exhibit closed in March. Our next special exhibit is called 'Hot Times in the City.' It's about Bushwick during the 1977 blackout."

Troy winced. "That's a terrible name for an exhibit."

"I know it." Darnell flashed Troy a toothy grin. "What about the Victorian project?"

"I remember you were doing some work on Henry Ward Beecher. I was just curious if you found anything new or especially interesting."

"We managed to track down the text of a bunch of his old sermons. There's a professor at Brooklyn College who is working on assembling a complete collection of his letters, and she contributed some things. My boss did a lot of the work on that."

"Can you pull any of the new research together?"

"Sure. It'll take me a couple of days, probably. You want to come back on Thursday?"

"Yeah, that'd be good." Troy contemplated mentioning

Finn. Darnell had been in Finn's undergrad class at Columbia, two years behind Troy. They'd all been a part of the same network of history students. Troy had long since fallen out of touch with most of them, Darnell being a notable exception, but Darnell still knew everyone and everything; he always seemed to have his finger on the pulse of the gossip. "I ran into Finn today."

Darnell raised an eyebrow. "Yeah? He looks good, right?"

Troy opted not to answer the question. But yes, he had looked damned good. "Do you know who he's working for now?"

"He's Loretta Kitteredge's research assistant."

Troy knew of her, mostly by reputation. "I've heard she's a real piece of work."

Darnell hooted with laughter. "Yeah. Rumor is she's no fun to work for. Eats assistants for breakfast. She's had more research assistants than you've had boyfriends, which is quite a feat."

"Ha."

Darnell squinted at Troy. "I take it our boy Finn was his usual charming self."

Troy sighed. "Yeah, he's still plenty pissed at me. He needs to get over himself. I am not the villain in his sad little tale of academic failure."

"Of course not."

Acknowledging the sarcasm in Darnell's voice, Troy said, "Hey, all I did was point out that there was a flaw in his dissertation research."

"In front of half his committee."

"I could not in good faith let him write that dissertation.

He was researching grass-roots movements but being really selective about the data. He underplayed the role the Women's Christian Temperance Union played in the ratification of the Nineteenth Amendment. You can't write about the women's movement without writing about the temperance movement. Do you know why women got the vote when they did? Not because they'd conquered sexism. The temperance movement knew that if women voted, they'd vote for Prohibition."

Darnell laughed. "You are such a pretentious asshole sometimes."

"I'm just saying."

"What was your dissertation on again?"

Troy grinned. "'The Homosexual Male in Gilded Age New York.'"

"Right. And that is in no way a self-serving topic."

"No. I will admit that my own homosexuality may have drawn me to the topic, but writing about men who died a hundred years ago is hardly self-serving."

"I thought Finn's research was interesting, for what it's worth. He was in the process of shifting focus when his funding got pulled. At the time, I told him I wanted to start the Darnell Movement. Hell, I'm gay and black. Ain't nobody stands up for me."

"Aw, Darnell. I adore you. You know that."

"I know. Now get out of here. All this reminiscing is making me sentimental."

Troy coughed. "Well, thanks for the stuff on Beecher. I'll see you Thursday."

"I'm meeting Mark for drinks when my shift ends tonight, if you want to come. He wants to check out the new gay sports bar in Chelsea. It's supposed to be really butch."

Troy hadn't been out in a while but wanted to spend the night with his books. That, and he was still preoccupied by Finn. "Nah, that's all right. I have to be up early to open the Brill House."

"Right, better get there at the crack of dawn so you can open your museum that no one comes to."

"Hey, we get some visitors."

"All right. Suit yourself. See you Thursday."

On his way to the circulation desk, Troy also grabbed Loretta Kitteredge's latest book.

When Troy got home, he shoved some leftovers in the microwave, and then sat on his couch and flipped through the Kitteredge book. She was what Troy considered a writer of pop history; she wrote books that appealed to the right number of people to get her on the *Times* bestseller list, but they didn't have a lot of scholarly value, at least not to Troy. This particular book was mostly about Margaret Corbin, a woman who fought in the Revolution. Kitteredge could tell a lurid tale—which, Troy supposed, explained her interest in Victoria Woodhull, who Troy remembered as being something of a nineteenth-century scandal magnet—but a lot of what he read only skimmed the surface without providing any real analysis.

He thumbed through the Woodhull biography next. The book had been published in the seventies and was pretty well worn. Troy skipped to the section of the book on the Beecher adultery trial. He was familiar with this particular story. Henry Ward Beecher had been a tremendously popular preacher in Brooklyn. In 1870, he had an affair with the wife of a friend, and word traveled. Woodhull published details in her newspaper and was arrested for sending obscene material through the mail. Beecher was exonerated, though the man he cuckolded sued, and a sensational trial followed, ending in a hung jury. It was one of those moments in American history that Troy had always been fascinated by. He was amazed by the hypocrisy exhibited by the stuffy, buttoned-up Victorians who condemned publicly acknowledging anything sexual but were getting into plenty of trouble behind closed doors. And here was Beecher, one of the most popular men in America and a moral crusader at that, getting a free pass to commit adultery.

Troy wondered if Woodhull really had spent much time in Brooklyn. It was likely she had, given her familiarity with the players in the scandal, most of whom resided in Brooklyn within a few blocks of the Brill House. Woodhull had been instrumental in blowing the lid off the scandal; she'd published details in the newspaper she and her sister produced.

Would she have ever met Brill or Cutler? He had no idea. If she had, could he then convince Finn to work with him? Troy had been thinking for a while that he would like some help with the research, and seeing Finn had gone a long way toward convincing him that, with his background researching this particular era of American history, Finn was the right man for the job. That, and Troy wanted to spend time with him again. Because though he could be surly and stubborn, he was also smart and logical and so very sexy. Troy and Finn had always had a good rapport—when they weren't pissing each other off, of course.

Research had been slow going thus far. Brill had kept journals, which Troy had been slowly working his way through. He'd sent them to the lab the KCHS used to preserve documents and had been getting the books back one at a time, after they'd been cataloged and scanned.

Brill hadn't written regularly. He tended to go through periods when he'd write a lot, sometimes more than once a day, and then he'd go for weeks with nary a word. Woodhull had given a speech in Brooklyn in 1871, which was a year Brill had been somewhat prolific. Maybe it was time to revisit that volume. It wasn't completely implausible for Brill and Woodhull to have crossed paths.

Troy put the Woodhull book down and went to retrieve his dinner from the microwave. He knew better than to think that he was looking for a connection between Brill and Woodhull solely out of academic curiosity.

Finn was still mad at him. It wasn't just because of the dissertation, as Darnell had implied. That was a big part of it—though Troy would go to his grave contending that he was in the right—but it was also years of rivalry and crimes against each other, maybe the most significant of which was that they'd slept together that time. Then that other time. And then again the last time Troy had seen Finn. Each time had involved explosive, mind-blowing sex, up there with the best sex Troy had ever had, and yet each time, Finn had gotten mad afterward, as if Troy had tricked him into it.

The truth was that Troy wanted another shot at Finn. And this time he was determined to make it good enough that Finn didn't regret it and resent him afterward. He wasn't sure exactly why this was the case—if part of it was the challenge or his crazy attraction to Finn or just wanting the really good sex to happen again—but he wanted it all the same, more now that he'd seen that Finn had looked so delicious, in his admittedly disheveled way.

And he wanted to get to the bottom of this mystery with Brill and Cutler. He knew he could put the pieces together himself, but two heads could solve it faster. Finn was good at research, and when he put his mind to it, he could find connections other people overlooked, his derailed dissertation notwithstanding. Troy had worked with him enough over the years that he knew this.

And, really, Troy thought, if he solved the mystery *and* got laid, well, two birds, one stone.

Troy finished dinner and quickly flipped through the rest of the books he'd checked out from the library, among them a really dry history of architecture in Brooklyn, a biography of a Civil War general, and—Troy's guilty pleasure—a pulp spy novel originally published in the sixties. He settled into the couch to start the novel.

Some rational part of Troy's brain knew this was a dream, which did not stop him from enjoying the sight of the naked man before him. There was a lot of muscle and skin on display. He thought at first that it was Finn, but then the man's face came into view. This man had kind of an unfortunate facial-hair situation, namely a mustache that was too long and some wispy sideburns. But his body might as well have been sculpted of clay for all its perfection. The sinewy muscles were those of a man who worked with his hands for a living, a man who worked in carpentry or construction.

The man hesitated at the foot of the bed before taking a step forward. "Are you sure about this, Teddy?"

Troy had never been more sure of anything. He wanted this man to fuck him. The overwhelming power of his desire surprised him. He looked down at himself to discover that he was also naked. That was a good step in the right direction. He slid back on the bed to make room for his mystery companion.

"Come here, Wash," Troy heard himself say.

What the hell kind of name was Wash? Well, if the smell of the man was anything to go by, it had been some time since he'd gotten near a shower, so there was that. Still, the smell was more intoxicating than off-putting, which reminded Troy of the time Finn had let him…

But then this Wash fellow was hovering over him. "Teddy," he murmured before dropping his head to kiss Troy.

Troy thought he should protest the mistaken identity more stridently, but then he lost himself in the kiss, in the simple sensation of lips sliding together. He felt something rising in his chest that felt an awful lot like emotion, like affection, like he really, deeply cared for this man he didn't remember ever seeing before.

And then Wash was inside him, and even though Troy thought they'd skipped a few steps, nothing hurt at all. It was all pleasure of the sort that spread through his whole body, making his toes curl and his fingers tangle in the sheets. *Oh, yeah. That's good.* He was content to let this stranger have his wicked way with him, as long as he kept sliding up against *that spot* and touched Troy *right there*, and he was mumbling and moaning and so close…

And then he was alone in his bed in the dark. He cried out in frustration that this dream had been cut short. He was still rock hard, so he took himself in hand. He tried to recall the dream, the way the other man had looked hovering over him, but instead images of Finn crept into his mind. He had a good store of memories, Finn's skin and hair and eyes, his long lanky body, his tangy sweet scent, the expression he made when he was about to lose his mind to orgasm. Troy stroked and remembered being with Finn and still felt something of that swell in his chest, the warmth for the other man that he'd felt in the dream.

He came on a long moan. Then he lay there for a moment, reflecting on the fact that he'd felt such strong emotion in his dream. It was an emotion more powerful than anything he'd remembered feeling before. Where had that come from?

Before he could spend much time contemplating it, he slipped back into sleep.

Chapter 3

Finn was working at Loretta's loft in SoHo—which meant he was doing some research and also he'd been told to keep an eye on her dog while she went out for a few hours—when his cell phone rang. At first, he planned to ignore it, but he looked at the caller ID out of curiosity. It wasn't a number he had programmed into the phone, but the 718 area code indicated the call was from Brooklyn. Finn thought he recognized it as the number of the Brill House, which meant Troy.

Hoping Troy had come up with something about Woodhull after all, he picked up his phone. "Hello?"

"I just made your day," Troy sing-songed, sounding especially smarmy.

"No, you didn't. If anything, the opposite is true. What do you want?"

"Touchy." Troy chuckled. "Look, I'm calling purely for professional reasons. I found two things that might interest you."

"Fine. What are they?" Finn knew he was being especially unpleasant, but he was tired and irritated. Maybe not all of his reasons for being upset with Troy were rational, but Finn was pretty determined to hold on to his anger. He liked his anger. Anger was safe.

"First, I found a photo of a woman who I'm pretty sure is Victoria Woodhull in this box from the KCHS archives. The photo itself has no identification on it, but I compared it to some others we had on file, and I'm all but certain. It's a Cabinet card, remarkably well preserved."

Finn thought that would be a pretty significant find.

Cabinet cards were sort of the nineteenth-century equivalent of a school picture, a popular kind of small portrait that people could pass around to friends and family. He'd seen a number of portraits of Woodhull, but a lot of the obscure ones Loretta had unearthed were blurry or else bad reproductions from prints for which the negatives had been destroyed. "Okay, thank you."

"I also have been going through the diaries of Theodore Cummings Brill, who I mentioned as being the first owner of this house. Here, let me read you the relevant section. This is from 1871." There was some static, then some shuffling of papers in the background of the call. "Okay, here we go. *Today I saw Mrs. Woodhull speak at the Brooklyn Academy of Music. I took a long walk along Montague Street afterward, trying to understand what I had heard. She is a vibrant speaker, and…*" Troy paused. "Well, it goes on at length. I also skipped ahead a little, it looks like Brill was impressed enough by the speech that he tried to make arrangements to meet her. Your supposition that she lived at the Brill House is still probably not accurate, but it *is* possible she and Brill met at least once. Most of Brill's many journals are at the lab for digital archiving, but I've been going through them as they come back, and I suspect that if I keep going, there will be more."

"This Brill is one of your ghosts, right?"

"Yes, I believe so."

Finn sighed. "All right. I'll come take a look at what you've found. Are you free tonight?"

Loretta came back not long after Finn got off the phone. She breezed in and asked for a report, so Finn related what Troy had dug up at the KCHS. She sat in the Queen Anne chair she sometimes used as a throne, occasionally nodding as he spoke.

"The photo Troy's got is a Cabinet card," Finn concluded. "He said it's well preserved."

"That certainly would be a great find, especially if it's not one anyone has seen before." Loretta pulled on one of her long dark curls. "This curator. You knew each other before I sent you to the house?"

"We went to college together."

"I take it he actually finished his PhD."

Finn huffed out a breath. "Yes. He was two years ahead of me in the program at NYU, so he was wrapping up his dissertation around the time my funding got pulled, and we had the same advisor, and… You know, it's kind of a long story, but, yes, Troy has a PhD in history. His particular area of expertise is Gilded Age New York. It pains me to admit this, but he might be a good resource for this project. I'm pretty sure Woodhull never set foot in the Brill House, but the main thrust of the museum is Brooklyn in the 1870s, so there might be some relevant background information to be found there."

"You should follow up with Troy, then, especially if he's able to bring us any new research on Woodhull. I'd really love to get my hands on the new photos, and I'd love if this project got the backing of the historical society."

"Yeah, I figured you'd say that."

Loretta frowned. "You don't like him much."

"It's not that I…" Finn shook his head. It was so hard to articulate his feelings on the matter of Troy Rafferty. Finn had been a freshman at Columbia the first time he'd encountered Troy, who at the time had a job in the Rare Book and Manuscript Library in Columbia's Butler Library.

Finn had thought Troy was smoking hot even then, but they'd started off on the wrong foot, with Troy giving Finn a hard time about checking out materials. Finn didn't know it at the time, but Troy was already the darling of all the professors Finn most wanted to take classes with, so their paths crossed all through that school year. It was a trend that continued when they both landed in the same PhD program a few years later. By then, Troy was Professor Feehan's wonder boy, so when Finn was first pitching his dissertation ideas, Feehan had solicited Troy's opinion. Finn had some grudging respect for Troy as a scholar, but it was around that same time that Finn's PhD started to unravel. Finn said to Loretta, "We've been rivals for a long time. You know how it is. Academia is competitive that way."

"Sure. Although I think you should make nice with the curator if it will help us with Victoria. You're not in academia anymore. You work for me."

Like Finn needed the reminder. Still, his interest was piqued by the mystery, and he thought it might be entertaining to see if there was anything to Troy's theories. On the other hand, it felt like there was too much between them to have it be that easy.

* * *

Troy found a somewhat disgruntled-looking Finn on the stoop outside the Brill House. His curly blond hair was tousled by the wind, and he was dressed casually in fitted jeans and a faded brown T-shirt. "Come in, come in," Troy said, hoping his natural exuberance would neutralize Finn's perpetually sour mood.

Finn walked into the lobby. "You're not open anymore, right?"

"No, we closed an hour ago, but I was working late

look, so he jogged a few paces ahead to catch up and walk next to Teddy.

They arrived back at the house, and Mrs. Morrison—clearly some sort of housekeeper—set them up with tea in the parlor. She put out a basket of sliced bread before retreating again, leaving them alone. Finn placed a slab of cheese on top of a slice of bread and tasted it. It was more tart than the cheddar he was used to, but it was delicious. He sipped the rather strong tea Mrs. Morrison had made.

Teddy smiled. "This will sound queer, but I do so enjoy watching you eat."

Finn laughed, not sure how to take that.

Teddy frowned and furrowed his brow. "Well, what I mean is, you take such relish in the things you do sometimes. I…admire your enthusiasm."

"Thank you," said Finn. "I enjoy sitting here with you like this. Or walking with you. Or doing anything with you." He almost backpedaled, thinking his gushing was too far over the line.

But Teddy looked thrilled. "Oh, yes. I quite like your company also. We have become great friends, have we not?"

"Yes, we…" He was aware of the fact that speaking too forwardly could get him into trouble or, worse, that he'd scare off Teddy.

"You looked so sad just then. Is something the matter?"

"No. Everything is fine."

Except everything was not fine, because an alarm started going off. Finn looked around the room, expecting to see fire, but there was nothing. Teddy sipped his tea calmly. Finn realized that it wasn't actually an alarm in the house…

But in his bedroom. He woke up with a start and hit

didn't especially like strawberries. At the same time, he felt happy to be walking with Teddy, the same sort of happiness he'd been feeling lately when he and Troy pored over some new piece of evidence together. Which was a problem, because Finn suspected that what he—or what Cutler, he supposed—felt for Teddy was love. And not just friendly, brotherly love, but full-on, lust-ridden, would-die-for-you love.

They chatted about the affairs of people they knew in common as they walked to the market. Most of the conversation was innocuous: Mr. Longwood did this, Miss Wright did that. What did Teddy think of the news about President Grant? Had he seen the article in the *Times* about Tennessee? They arrived at the market, and Finn/Cutler beelined for the cheese counter, where he picked out a nice-looking hunk of cheddar. A few minutes later, he found Teddy, who was holding a box.

Mischievously, Teddy said, "They had the little strawberry pastries."

"You devil!" Finn/Cutler laughed. "Well, I look forward to eating them with you."

They walked back to the house. Finn sometimes fell a few paces behind on the pretense of admiring a rose bush or a house he'd never noticed before, but really to get a better look at Teddy's ass, which was a fine one indeed. Watching Teddy was arousing, but as they walked, the feeling seemed to be coupled with shame too. The depth of that shame surprised Finn. The part of Finn's mind that was still his own sympathized with that feeling, had felt some measure of it himself as a teenager, but he was surprised by how vehement and intense this shame felt, how much Cutler hated himself for lusting after Teddy. The shame overrode his desire to

Chapter 9

Finn fell asleep reading Cutler's journal. That was what must have happened, because what else could explain him suddenly walking down a cobblestone street? It looked a lot like the streets near the Brill House, only there were no cars parked at the curb, no electric street lights, and no hum from the nearby Brooklyn-Queens Expressway. He looked down and noticed that he was wearing a rather dapper brown suit.

He looked up again and saw that a man was walking toward him. This man was quite handsome, with curly, reddish-brown hair, a compact body, a beard, and a wide smile. "Hullo, Mr. Cutler!" the man said cheerily.

"Cheers, Teddy," Finn heard himself say. "Where have you been this morning?"

"I took a walk down to Montague Street. I thought I would see about getting tickets to that play they are showing at the Academy of Music. Shakespeare, it turns out. *The Merchant of Venice.*"

"Did you succeed?"

"I did!" He reached into his pocket and produced two pieces of paper. "Would you like to accompany me? The show is the Tuesday after next."

"I would love nothing more." Finn felt warmth spread through his chest. If he didn't know better, he'd think he'd just been asked out on a date.

Teddy smiled. Finn knew this was *the* Teddy, Theodore Cummings Brill, in the flesh, as real as Troy or Janice was in his waking life.

Or maybe more like Troy, because Finn found his thoughts wandering toward the erotic. His desire to get Mr.

Brill naked was acute. Finn wondered how much of this was just his own horny, undersexed mind—though not so undersexed lately—and how much of this was what Cutler would have felt, gazing at a man he found this good-looking, gazing at his good friend or possibly his lover.

He said, "I do very much like *The Merchant of Venice*. I know it is a ridiculous play, with all the disparate parts that do not really fit together, but a good cast can make it entertaining." He considered. "I have always liked Shakespeare. I saw Edwin Booth star as Hamlet a few years ago."

"Yes. Your uncle told me when we had dinner last week that he saw the Booth brothers in *Julius Caesar* in 1864. That seems quite remarkable."

The part of his brain that was still Finn's thought that was astonishing. He wondered what it must have been like to see John Wilkes Booth on stage. Booth was famous even before he shot Lincoln, one of the best-known and best-loved actors in the country. He must have been something to have gained that kind of notoriety in the days before even photographs could be mass produced.

Finn also registered that they were walking down the street.

"Where are you off to?" asked Teddy.

"I thought I might go to the market near City Hall. I know you like for Mrs. Morrison to do most of the shopping, but I was wanting a good sharp cheese to go with the bread she made. None was to be found in your kitchen."

Teddy chuckled. "You and your stomach! Well, let us walk together. I have a mind to buy something sweet. Maybe those pastries you like. The ones with the strawberries."

Finn felt his mouth water, which was odd because he

the button on his alarm clock. When he sat up, Cutler's journal slid off his lap. Finn moved to pick it up and noticed that it had fallen open. He picked up the book and read the exposed page.

My days are full of longing for that which I will never be able to touch, and I know not how to reconcile what is going on in my head with what I know to be proper. The worst part is I am starting to suspect that perhaps my dear Teddy regards me similarly. But how can that be? He is everything pure and clean. 'Tis I who am a monster.

Finn closed the book. He wondered if he should be happy for this discovery or annoyed that Troy had been right all along.

* * *

Troy and Darnell were having a drink at Joyce, a pub in Brooklyn Heights with a vaguely *Dubliners* theme. Darnell was explicating some story he'd read, but Troy was only half paying attention. He was really waiting for Finn, whom he had invited to join them.

The man himself breezed into the bar ten minutes into Darnell's rant on class and privilege. "Thanks for meeting me," Finn said as he sat down. "Hi, Darnell."

Darnell didn't look bothered that his lecture had been interrupted. He waved at Finn. "Christopher Finnegan, as I live and breathe. Long time, no see."

"I saw you last week," said Finn, but he smiled. Then he looked at Troy. "So I had this dream."

"Wow. Not even a, 'Hey, Darnell, how are you?' or an apology for interrupting what was most definitely a thrilling discussion on an important issue in historiography?"

Finn shrugged. "Pretty sure we had this discussion last time I saw you." To Troy, he added, "Early twentieth century thought? Class privilege? That book by Butterfield?"

Troy nodded.

"I'm all caught up, then. So about this dream."

Troy noticed Finn was nearly breathless. "Was I in it?"

"No." Finn flagged down a waitress and ordered a beer. He glanced at Darnell and grinned. "So how are you, D? How's Mark?"

Troy was annoyed by the deflection. He crossed his arms and glared at Finn.

"You can ask Mark yourself if he ever gets off work," Darnell said. "He was supposed to be here fifteen minutes ago. And you're changing the subject. What's this about a dream? I hope it was really raunchy."

Bless Darnell.

Finn took a deep breath. "Well, I—"

He was saved by Darnell's boyfriend, Mark, who came into the bar then. He gave Darnell a kiss on the cheek before greeting Troy and taking a seat. He seemed to notice Finn was there almost as an afterthought. "Whoa, hey, Finn!" he said. "How's it going? I heard you were working for Loretta Kitteredge. I'm amazed you don't have more bite marks."

At Troy's raised eyebrows, Finn coughed. "Yeah. I might have to go back tonight, actually. But anyway. I was reading Cutler's journal last night. I fell asleep and had a dream that, let's just say, confirmed your suspicions about Cutler."

"What were your suspicions?" Darnell asked.

Troy had given him the short version, that he thought the Brill House was haunted by the two men who had been killed there, but not much else. "One of Brill's tenants, this guy Cutler, was gay," said Troy.

"In a passage I found in the journal," Finn said, "he laments that he's attracted to Brill but unable to act on it, primarily because he's terribly ashamed of that impulse and thinks Brill is an innocent virgin. That's not what he says, exactly, but that's the subtext."

"That is interesting," said Troy. "And funny, because I get the impression Brill was anything but virginal."

"I don't understand what a dream has to do with any of this," Darnell said. "Was there at least sex in the dream?"

"No," said Finn.

"Really?" asked Troy. "Because I had a dream a few weeks ago that was really hot."

"That's nice, Troy," said Finn.

"No, wait, hear me out. In the dream, I was in Brill's head, and my most fervent desire was to have a man I thought of as Wash, who I have since discovered was Cutler. And by have, I mean that I wanted him to fuck me."

"Is that not always your most fervent desire?" asked Mark.

Finn looked puzzled. "In my dream, I was Cutler. Or I was in his head."

"Interesting," said Troy. "But no sex?"

"We went shopping."

Darnell laughed. "Of course!"

"These were just dreams, though," Finn said.

Troy looked at him. Finn looked at his beer and chewed on his lower lip. "I think there's a little more going on," Troy said.

"Right," said Mark. "You're still on the ghost kick."

Troy tapped Finn's shoulder to get his attention. "How

else do you explain the incident with the chaise?"

"What incident with the chaise?" Darnell asked.

"I don't," said Finn. He downed the rest of his beer. There was a buzzing noise, and Finn pulled a cell phone from his pocket. "Fantastic. It's Loretta."

He answered the phone, and Troy heard a woman's voice on the other end, though the words were hard to make out. As the phone call progressed, the woman's voice grew increasingly irritable, and Finn looked increasingly frustrated. He gave her mostly one-word responses and got yelled at in return. He concluded with, "Yes. I can be there in twenty minutes or so if I leave now." He ended the call and looked Troy. "Well. I just thought you'd find the dream thing interesting. I have to go back to Loretta now. See you guys later."

"You just got here," Troy said. "We haven't eaten yet." It frustrated Troy to have so little time with Finn, and not only because he wanted to explore this dream thing more.

"The mothership calls me back," said Finn. "Some other time."

"Are you in some kind of trouble?" Troy asked.

"No." Finn stood and hoisted his bag over his shoulder. "Loretta was playing phone tag with some women's studies professor at the University of Chicago all day. She finally managed to connect, and they put together that they have a bunch of conflicting information on Woodhull. Or, not even conflicting, just some letters and things Woodhull wrote that contradict one of Loretta's theories, so now she's having a crisis. I'm sorry guys. I really do have to go."

He briefly touched Troy's shoulder. Then he turned and walked out of the bar.

Troy half expected to hear a sarcastic comment, but instead, Darnell said, "What happened with the chaise, Helen?"

Troy grinned. "Finn tried to use it as a tool of seduction. I took him home with me instead."

Mark rolled his eyes. "You had sex with Finn. Again."

"Yes, I did, and I will not apologize for it, because it was good, and I fully intend to do it again, just as soon as I can get him to sit still for more than ten minutes."

"You do remember that bit where he hates you," said Mark.

"Oh sure. He hates me so much that he called me this morning wanting to meet tonight just to tell me about a dream he had."

"Uh-oh," said Mark. "I don't like the sound of all that affection in your voice. You might be starting to actually like him too."

Troy had never not liked Finn, but he understood what he was supposed to say here and didn't want to give away too much to Darnell and Mark anyway. "Oh, sorry," he said. "What I meant to say was that he hates me so much that he made me come three times the other night."

Darnell laughed. "Well. At least you've got your priorities worked out."

Chapter 10

When Finn arrived at the Brill House the following Monday, the first thing he said once he was settled into one of the chairs in Troy's office was, "Do you happen to have photos of our alleged ghosts?"

"As a matter of fact." Troy pulled an envelope out of his desk. He opened it to reveal a few prints protected by cardboard. "There are dozens of photos of Brill," he said. "The bulk of them are from when he was younger, and he's featured in a lot of family portraits, but he sat for a few portraits when he was older too, after he moved to the Brill House. We think this one is from 1873 or so." He handed the photo to Finn.

Finn looked at it for a long time. Troy had already spent a lot of time staring at that particular photo and thought it showed Brill at his best. He looked calm and relaxed. He had an unblemished face, light hair, and a neatly trimmed beard. The photo cut him off midchest, but his wide shoulders were there, and he had a physical strength that wasn't completely hidden underneath the dark suit he wore.

"He's a good-looking man," Finn said.

"I thought so too. I have some wider-angle photos upstairs. He was a chubby kid, but he lost some weight when he hit his thirties. The timing of that seems to correspond with when he moved to Brooklyn. I'm guessing those were leaner years in more ways than one."

Finn handed the photo back, so Troy pulled out another. "This is Cutler in the early 1870s. There aren't many photos of him. He was not nearly as well off as Brill, so photographic portraits, though not outrageously expensive at this time, were not something he could really afford often."

Finn spent a lot of time looking at this photo as well. It was a wide shot of Cutler in which he looked polished but a little frazzled. His dark hair had been neatly combed, and he had a goatee that looked carefully maintained. He was tall and rangy, muscular but thin to an almost unhealthy-looking degree. The first impression was that he was a bit of a dandy, but there was something unsettled in his eyes, something raw and a little angry.

"He's so thin," Finn said.

"Which is a shame, because I think if he ate a few hearty meals, he'd be really handsome. Don't you think?"

Finn turned his head to the side and contemplated the photo again. "Sure, I can see that." He handed the photo back.

"The museum catalogs indicate that there are a few later photos of Cutler and a photo of Brill and Cutler together, but I haven't run across them yet."

"A photo of them together would be a real find, I suppose."

"And yet somehow I doubt that it'll show them with their arms thrown around each other in happy domestic bliss."

Finn nodded. "Well, unfortunately, I haven't had much time to read this week. It's just been too busy. Do you mind if I take some time now so we actually have things to talk about?"

Troy had been hoping for a little more from Finn. He wanted to talk about dreams and sex and a few of his latest theories on the crime. But Finn looked exhausted. "Okay."

Finn seemed grateful, smiling and relaxing his

shoulders. He took a large envelope out of his bag and slid Cutler's journal from it.

Troy picked up the volume of Brill's journal he'd most recently gotten back from the lab and began to read as well.

They sat together reading silently for a half hour. Troy read a passage he found tense and emotional. He stared at the page, surprised, until he realized Finn was trying to get his attention.

"Oh, tell me what you found," said Troy.

"You first."

"If you insist." Troy cleared his throat. "This is the 1874 journal. September ninth. Brill says, *Wash has seemed out of sorts for days. He's been short with me and often he leaves a room the moment I enter it.* Blah, blah, Brill is concerned, blah. Then he says, *I saw him sitting in the parlor today. He was absorbed in a book and did not hear me come in, so he could not leave before I had the opportunity to speak with him. I cleared my throat and said, 'Are you cross with me?'*

"*'No,' he responded.*

"*'Then why do you persist in dodging me whenever I am in your presence?' said I.*

"*He looked quite distressed. He said, 'I cannot be in your presence anymore. It is too painful.'*

Finn sat up straighter in his chair. "Wait, listen to this. *It is difficult to stay away from someone when you live in the same house, but I find that I can no longer be in dear Teddy's company without fear that I will expose how I feel.* Hmm, I wonder if…" Finn flipped the page.

Troy said, "Brill continues, *I sat next to him on the sofa. I said, 'It is painful for me that you are upset with me.' The truth is that I have been missing him, even though he lives in my house.*

"*'I am not upset with you,'* he said, *'I am upset with myself. I do not know how to act anymore. There is something terribly wrong with me.'* I was confused and yet hopeful. It is so hard sometimes to say what we feel in our hearts, especially when we know it is not something Society deems appropriate. I have wondered for some time whether Wash feels the way I do about our friendship, if he knows how indispensable it has become to me.*

"I said, 'Wash, nothing is wrong with you.' His anguish was evident. I reached out and touched his face, hoping to be comforting. He closed his eyes and leaned into my hand. After a long moment, he opened his eyes again. 'This,' he said. 'This is wrong.'

"I leaned closer. My greatest desire was to kiss him, to comfort him, to take his pain away. 'What is wrong?' I asked.

"'This,' he said. Then he kissed me." Troy grinned.

"Cutler says, *I can't help but think I am in more peril than ever. For today, my darling Teddy and I kissed. It was at once the greatest and most terrible moment of my life.* He has a real flair for the dramatic, if that wasn't obvious."

Troy laughed. "Can you imagine? I keep wondering what it must have been like to be Brill. I've gathered from his journal that he had a little bit of experience with men before he met Cutler. That's kind of amazing given that sodomy was still illegal in New York, and Brill was a bit of a Goody Two-shoes otherwise." Troy glanced at the journal lying open on his desk. "I feel like being gay is risky enough now. At least I won't be committing a criminal act the next time I let you fuck me."

"Let me…" Finn looked down at the book in his lap and then shook his head.

Troy knew Finn was aware that not just the actual act of sodomy was illegal. This was the era of Comstock and obscenity laws, not to mention the fact that places where homosexuals congregated got raided all the time. "I think it was 1903 that the Ariston Hotel Baths were raided. Some of the men brought up on sodomy charges got twenty years in prison. Twenty years!"

"I wonder if the danger was part of the appeal."

Troy thought about that. "Maybe in some cases, but not here." He pointed to the journal. "I think this is more a case of not being able to help oneself. I mean, have you ever wanted someone like that? So badly that the risk didn't matter? In Brill and Cutler's time, there was a very real risk of public condemnation and either prison time or being exiled to an insane asylum. In the modern era, we have AIDS."

"Point taken."

"Victorian homosexuals didn't identify as such, really. The late nineteenth century saw the beginnings of gay resorts and dance halls on the Bowery and that sort of thing, places for men who wanted to be with other men to congregate, and of course there had been male prostitutes in the city since it was founded. But most gay men of the era had sex with other men but not relationships. And yet what we're seeing here is, I think, two men who have fallen in love with each other but are terrified of acting on it, Cutler probably more so than Brill. Because he has no experience with it, he doesn't know gay relationships can exist. You and I know that romantic love between two men is possible, and we know because we've studied history that love has always been part of the human experience, but Brill and Cutler would have had no frame of reference for this."

Finn sniffed. "Love? I thought you were skeptical about it really being love if they weren't sleeping together."

"Maybe I've changed my mind." Troy scratched his chin. "Cutler was thirty-four years old in 1874. He'd never had sex because he couldn't initiate it, or so I extrapolate based on what you've told me you've read. He wouldn't have known how or that he could."

"Yeah. That's my guess also."

"Whereas I basically have to go, 'Hey, Finn, we're alone here,' and waggle my eyebrows, and bam!" Troy clapped his hands for emphasis.

"I'm not having sex with you in the museum."

"Says the man who wanted to give me a blowjob on the antique chaise longue upstairs."

"I don't know what got into me. I plead temporary insanity."

Troy thought of the ghosts and smiled. "Anyway, I applaud Cutler for his bravery, making the first move on Brill. That must have taken guts. Based on the passages you've read to me, he seems kind of uptight. Maybe what he needed was a little sin and sodomy."

"Of course you would think that. Isn't that your motto?"

"Whatever, Finn. You are hardly a virgin." He looked down at the journal and flipped a couple of pages. "You know, you never answered my question."

"What question?" Finn's annoyance was apparent in his voice. When Troy looked up at him, he was scowling.

Troy found he liked that Finn could be so prickly. He was enormously entertaining when he was irritated. "Have you ever wanted someone so badly that any risk or danger involved in your coupling didn't matter?"

"I don't..." Then he went white, which Troy had not expected. He stood up. "I'll be right back." He shuffled out of the room.

Curious, Troy got up to follow him. He hadn't sensed the ghosts, but he wondered if Finn had, if that was what had spooked him. He got to the hallway in time to see Finn disappear into the men's room. Troy walked there slowly, figuring he'd give Finn a minute, but then he barged in. "Are you all right?"

Finn stood at the mirror, his hand on his forehead, a few stray drops of water trickling off his nose. "Yeah," he said shakily.

"Did you have a ghost encounter?"

"No." He shook his head and dropped his hand. "No, nothing like that. I just got suddenly dizzy. And I realized something kind of unpleasant."

"What's that?"

"You. You annoy the crap out of me most of the time. I've forgiven you for most of the old shit, but you're still *you*. You're pushy and nosy and opinionated and stubborn. You make jokes at inappropriate times, and you piss me off like few people I know. And yet I still want you enough to push mountains aside to get to you."

That took Troy aback. "Really?"

"Shut up. You know how attractive you are."

The funny thing was that Troy knew somehow that his relative attractiveness was not the only thing going on here. Troy had lusted after a number of hot men over the years, but he wouldn't have crawled over hot coals to get to them, which is how he sometimes felt about Finn. He tried to put himself in Brill's shoes. Would he have risked his home, his livelihood, his life, for this man standing before him? Troy thought he might. Maybe that wasn't love, exactly; after all, Brill only wanted a taste. He had no way of conceptualizing a true relationship, a lifetime of companionship and sex, with Cutler. Troy had the benefit of one hundred and forty years of progress pushing him into this moment. The risk wasn't nearly so great. He could kiss Finn right now, and his world would keep on turning as it always had.

So he kissed Finn, who responded enthusiastically, snaking his hands around Troy's neck, getting his fingers tangled in Troy's hair. Troy put his hands on Finn's waist and parted his lips, and everything was at war in his body, pulling him inexorably toward Finn. But still he wanted to hold back, aware that they were in a public restroom and that Genevieve and Peter the librarian were still rattling around the building somewhere.

Troy pulled away slightly. "This is not just sexual attraction."

"What?" Finn furrowed his brow but then leaned in for another kiss.

Troy dodged him. Finn had only confessed to a sexual attraction, it was true, but Troy thought there was something more here. "What's going on between you and me. Not just sex. I mean, it is, partly, of course it is, but if that were it, we'd have more self-control."

"What are you talking about?" Finn raised his eyebrows.

"Never mind." It didn't seem worth it to make the argument. He stepped away from Finn. The frustrating thing was Finn was always putting up walls, shutting down, making his heart unavailable. Troy wondered if all of Finn's hostility, which seemed to be increasingly hollow as time went on, was just another kind of wall. "I just came to see if you were okay."

"I'm fine. Let's go back."

"Would you like to move this to my place?" Troy

lowered his voice, trying to sound alluring.

Finn paused at the door to the men's room and turned around. "I think we'd better not."

"Right. Sure."

"Troy…"

"It's fine. Let's get back to work."

Finn pressed his lips together. "I know you want to talk about this, but I'm not really ready. I need some time to process… all this." He gestured at the air between them. "Can we table it for now and talk about Brill and Cutler."

"Of course."

Finn sighed. "You sound pissed. Are you pissed?"

Troy wasn't. He was disappointed, but he wasn't angry. "No. You're probably right. Sex will just distract us from the mission at hand." He'd tried to lighten his tone.

Finn only nodded.

They walked back to Troy's office together. Finn said, "What do you think this course of events does for your suicide theory?"

"I'm not ruling anything out until we see the police report."

"Because here's the thing. They kiss, right? Let's assume a relationship develops." Finn held the door open for Troy on the way back into the office. "Four years later, they kill themselves? I don't think so. It would happen right away, when the shame is the greatest. Four years is too long an interlude."

"You're probably right. Brill doesn't strike me as suicidal." Troy sat in his chair.

"I wish I could say the same for Cutler. Parts of his

journal are pretty melancholy. It's like… Imagine the shame you felt when you first figured out you were gay or when you first came out, or what have you, and then multiply it by a thousand, and you might get close to the intensity of Cutler's self-loathing."

"So Cutler could have killed Brill and then killed himself."

Finn tilted his head and wrinkled his nose. "Eh, that doesn't seem right either. I don't think Cutler ever meant Brill any harm. I mean, there are some incredibly sappy passages where Cutler goes on and on about how wonderful Brill is. Wait, hang on a sec, I'll demonstrate." He picked Cutler's journal back up and flipped through the pages. "Ah, here we go. '*Teddy came into the parlor while I was reading this afternoon. He brought me a cup of tea and a strawberry tart. I asked why, and he said he merely wanted to bring a little sunshine to my day. I wanted to say that he did not need to bring me tea and pastries to do that. His presence in a room makes it infinitely brighter. I thanked him. He sat on the sofa across from me with no tea or pastry of his own. He leafed through my book as I ate. I watched him. I found that looking at him made me happier than I have felt for a very long time. His face is pleasant.*' Blah blah. He goes on at some length here, describing Brill's appearance. Reddish-brown hair, light eyes, pale skin, freckles, stocky body, all apparently things that appeal to Cutler."

"Sure. I was always a fan of gingers."

Finn gave Troy a long look, his expression mostly neutral but his eyes clouding a little with annoyance. "Uh, right. Anyway, it's not the mere fact of his describing Brill's appearance but the loving way he does it. My point is that I believe Cutler really cherished Brill, valued their friendship, before they'd even developed a relationship, so although

I wouldn't put it past Cutler to do himself in, I don't see him ever intentionally causing physical harm to Brill." Finn looked at the journal where it now lay in his lap. He flipped through a few pages. "I guess that could change."

"No, I see your point. I'm interested to know how this develops."

"Me too."

By some unspoken mutual agreement, they went back to reading their respective journals. Sometime later, Troy stopped and said, "Funny how we should come across an account of the same event at the same time."

"Coincidence. Frustratingly, Cutler apparently didn't feel it was necessary to detail anything that happened in the subsequent days. The next entry is in December and mostly whines about the drudgery of shoveling snow."

"Yeah. Brill is mostly silent on that too. Maybe nothing happened."

"Maybe."

That seemed unlikely.

"You know," said Troy. "I think I'm about done for tonight. I'm pretty tired. All the words are kind of swimming around on the page."

"Oh, sure, okay. I might go home and read some more, if that's okay with you."

"Of course."

They each packed up. Troy felt a bit deflated. He considered trying to ask Finn back to his apartment again, but Finn started mumbling about needing to get home to talk to Janice about something. Troy locked up, said good-night to Finn, and went home.

* * *

Finn got home and went straight to his room. He changed into a T-shirt and boxers and got in bed. He lay awake for a while, thinking about Troy. He thought about the way his libido kicked into high gear in Troy's presence. He thought about Troy's muscular chest, his strong thighs, his dark hair, those stupid Clark Kent glasses. He thought about the last few weeks and acknowledged to himself that he had enjoyed spending time with Troy to an extent, that maybe he liked arguing with him and talking with him and spending time in the same room, even when they weren't fucking. And what did that mean?

He drifted off eventually and slid into a dream in which he was seated on a sofa next to a man who he thought at first was Troy until he blinked and realized he was, in fact, sharing cushion space with Theodore Cummings Brill. He heard only about half of what Brill was saying, some explanation about how he, Finn, was not a flawed individual, that, in fact, everything about him was perfect. Brill reached over and touched Finn's face. Finn closed his eyes and leaned into the touch. He craved this man, wanted his touch, wanted his hands all over. He said, "This is wrong." When Brill asked what was wrong, Finn gave in to his basest desires and kissed him.

It took Finn a moment to realize he was dreaming in Cutler's head again. He deepened the kiss and thought about how different it was to kiss Brill than it was to kiss Troy, although it was the same in some ways too. They tasted similarly of herbal tea and something unidentifiable yet masculine, but they smelled different. In recent years, Troy had taken to wearing some cologne with a spicy kick to it, masculine but artificial. Brill was earthier and smelled a little of cigar smoke, not to mention that he was hairier, didn't have Troy's persnickety need for everything to be just so. Finn was aware he was dreaming, but he was startled by how rough Teddy's beard felt against his face. He'd never really been into hairy guys and had never kissed anyone with a full beard before.

Soon, thoughts of Troy receded, and he found himself kissing Teddy deeply, all of his feelings swimming forward, his love and affection for Teddy manifesting itself as a tightness in his chest.

Then he felt horrified. He'd just done something that could cost him everything. When they broke apart, Teddy looked at him with such earnestness, it broke Finn's heart.

"I don't know how to do this," Finn said.

Teddy laughed, joy ringing out of his voice. "Nor I, but I believe we will be able to work it out together."

* * *

Troy had taken a volume of Brill's diary home with him, intending to read, but he felt tired and sad and not really up for it. Instead, he peeled off his clothes and climbed into bed.

He was asleep almost instantly and soon found himself in a dream in which he was sitting on a sofa very much like the one in the parlor at the Brill House. He was seated on said sofa next to a man he recognized now as Wash. He saw his hand reach over and caress Wash's face. "There's nothing wrong with you, Wash," he heard himself say.

"This. This is wrong," Wash said.

"What is wrong?"

Then they were kissing. It was a hell of a kiss. He'd thought briefly of the history of every man he'd ever kissed and each of those prior kisses paled in comparison to this one, tender as it was, electric as it was. Troy parted his lips and sucked on Wash's tongue. There was not a thing wrong with this, Troy thought, just two men, sitting on a couch, making out with each other.

The sofa on which they sat morphed into the chaise, and Troy was then making out with Finn on it, and his body was hard and screaming for release. He raked his hands through Finn's hair, all those blond curls he loved, and he felt a swell of emotion. Everything swam around in his head, pictures flashing, Wash then Finn, then everything red and warm. Troy cared deeply for the man whose body was under his hands, though he was confused for a moment about whose mind he inhabited, whether he was Theodore Brill or Troy Rafferty, until he looked down and saw Finn beneath him, arching toward him, crying out, "Troy."

Then they were in the Bobst Library at NYU, hidden somewhere in the stacks. Finn was shouting at him, working himself into a froth over something Troy had said to him. "And then Feehan keeps saying, 'Go talk to Rafferty, he knows what's what,' because you're now the goddamn expert on everything that ever happened ever."

"You can't blame me for that," Troy said. "I never said that, Feehan did."

Hadn't they had this argument a hundred times? Troy couldn't recall if they'd argued this way so often in real life or in dreams.

Finn said, "Well, here I am talking to you. I haven't learned a goddamn thing about whatever it is you're supposed to be an expert in, but I have learned that you are about the most arrogant, annoying, son of a—"

"Instead of shouting at me, you could let me help you."

"Fuck off, Troy."

It was like being stuck in a home movie. This was a memory farmed from his mind somewhere, brought forth and tangled with everything else. This wasn't borne of his imagination; it was a moment he knew but hadn't thought about in a long time. And it was so very real.

"You're investigating the intersection of various civil rights movements at the end of the nineteenth century. I'm researching Gilded Age New York, particularly from the perspective of an overlooked population. It seems like we should have more common ground."

Finn stared at him. "I hate when you're rational."

"Maybe if you got over yourself, you wouldn't hate me so much."

"I don't hate you."

"You have a funny way of showing that. Anyway, I think there could be some common space where our research intersects, and I'd be happy to share some of what I've found with you."

Finn looked at Troy for a long time. "You think we have common ground? I'll show you common ground."

And then Finn was on him, pressing Troy's back into a bookcase as they kissed. Troy felt something burst, some breath he'd been holding popping like a bubble, and he groaned and pressed his growing erection into Finn's hip.

Finn kissed him like he was starving and his only sustenance could be found in Troy's mouth. Troy wanted to scream with the sheer joy of it. Finn's hand trailed down his spine and then grabbed his ass, and he could feel Finn's hard cock through his pants, and it was starting to look like they were just going to fuck right here in the stacks—long a fantasy of Troy's—but then, just as quickly as they'd come together, Finn pushed away.

They stood there, staring at each other, panting.

"Fuck you," Finn said.

"Hey, *you* kissed *me*."

Finn shook his head. "There are not words for how much you frustrate me."

"Likewise. That was about the least romantic first kiss ever."

"First kiss? Only kiss. That was a huge mistake. I don't know what I was thinking."

Troy took a step toward Finn, whose body went slack. He dropped his arms, and Troy could see his guard drop too, his resistance crumbling like an old wall. Troy took Finn's face in his hands and brought their lips back together again, this time with more tenderness and affection. He moved his mouth slowly and savored, learning what Finn tasted like—mostly like the black licorice candies he had lately taken to sucking on—but Troy also tasted and smelled dusty books and aftershave. Finn was a champion kisser, and Troy imagined this would be as all things were with Finn; when he really put his mind to something, when he concentrated and worked, he excelled.

Finn grabbed Troy. There was less urgency in the kiss this time, more curiosity. When at last the kiss began to fade, Finn pulled away, keeping his hands on Troy's waist.

"I would like to point out that I'm making out in the stacks of a university library with Troy fucking Rafferty."

"Yeah." Troy felt dizzy from the kiss, unable to really form words. Because, shit, he had really liked kissing Finn.

Finn pulled his hands away and smiled ruefully. "Well,"

he said. He glanced at the shelf next to him. "Oh." He ran his hand over a book that had the title *Suffragist Discourse* printed on it in gold leaf. He pulled it off the shelf then held it up. "Guess I got what I came for." Then he walked away.

Troy wished he could have said the same.

The rest of his dreams were a confusion of images, flashes of sensation, what it felt like to kiss Finn, to kiss Wash, to touch each man's skin, to have each man inside him, and when he woke up the next morning, he had no idea how to sort through any of it.

What he did know was that he was probably now in over his head with Finn, if he was having dreams about their first kiss, all those years before. His feelings for Finn and Teddy's feelings for Wash were tangled up in his head, but Troy wondered if they were really so different.

Chapter 11

Finn gazed around Loretta's apartment, letting his mind wander. He was pretty sure the space had, given the building's architecture and location, once been a garment sweatshop of some sort. He could picture long rows of sewing machines with women hunched over them. He was even sweating a little bit as Loretta herself sauntered into the room. She wore a purple caftan and seemed oblivious to the fact that the sun shining through the west-facing windows was making the whole apartment unbearably hot.

"Darling, I need you to go to the deli and get me a sandwich," she said. "Not the cheap place on the corner but the nice deli on Prince Street."

"Are you interested in any of what I've found this week? I typed up a summary but haven't printed it out yet."

She pulled over the Queen Anne chair and draped herself on it. "Naturally. Have you made any progress with Colonel Blood?"

"Some." Finn turned to his laptop and pulled up the file he'd made notes in. He was about to give Loretta the highlights when his cell phone rang. He reached for it by instinct and realized only after he had it in his hand that it was probably bad form.

"Who is it, dear?" Loretta asked.

"Troy," he said. Of course it was Troy. "He's my contact at the Kings County Historical Society."

"Then answer it."

He braced himself and answered.

"Great news!" said Troy. "My NYPD contact just

faxed me the police report."

Finn glanced at Loretta and wondered how he'd get away with discussing the ghosts in front of her. "That's good. Anything interesting?"

"Yes, actually. It's a little hard to read, but it seems to me that the evidence indicates a murder, not a suicide. Or perhaps it was a murder intended to look like a murder-suicide."

Finn thought that sounded like it would require more explanation than he had time to sit through just then, especially with Loretta hovering. "Listen, unless you have something Woodhull-related, this is not a great time to talk."

"Oh. Okay. Can I see you tonight?"

Finn looked at Loretta, who was writing some notes in a notebook she seemed to have produced out of thin air.

"Yeah, all right," Finn said. "It might be late, though."

"Let's meet at my place, then."

Finn wondered if that was a good idea. It had been a couple of days since the night they'd read about Brill and Cutler's first kiss. The previous night, he had put Cutler's journal aside hoping to be able to think about something else. Despite the distractions of a dumb TV movie and then a game of hearts with Janice, all he'd been able to think of was Troy. If Troy was on his mind this much, the odds of them hooking up again if Finn went over there tonight seemed pretty high.

Although, Troy hadn't even suggested anything of the sort. He wanted to talk about the police report. And it made sense to meet at Troy's apartment if it was going to be late, since many public spaces would be closed.

"Sure," Finn said. "I'll come by tonight."

Finn hung up and glanced at Loretta. She scribbled another note and looked up.

"What did he have to say?"

"He has no further Woodhull news. He's been researching something related to the Brill House and wanted to share his findings. He thought I'd be interested."

"That's nice, dear. Let's talk more about Victoria after lunch. I want that sandwich they have with the roasted red peppers and artichoke hearts. Be a darling." She handed Finn a twenty.

* * *

Finn looked exhausted. He sat on Troy's couch staring into the cup of coffee Troy had made him and still swayed in his seat like he was about to pass out.

"Do you want to take a nap or something?" Troy asked. "We can do this some other time."

"I'm fine. Tell me what the report says. I've been wondering all day."

Troy smiled. He picked the faxed pages up from where he'd left them on the coffee table. "Murder weapon was a two-shot derringer, which suggests premeditation to me. Brill took a bullet to the chest, which nicked his heart, according to the autopsy. He bled out on the floor of the bedroom upstairs. Cutler was shot in the head, probably died instantly. The derringer was found in his hand."

"Wait, let me interrupt you for a second," Finn said, holding up his hand. "I can tell by the expression on your face that you're about to twist this all around on its ear, so tell me again why your initial suspicion was suicide."

"I don't know," Troy said. "I say that with all honesty. When I first started looking into historical owners of the house, I'd already had a few ghost sightings, so I was thinking about who the ghosts might have been. I found that story in the *Times* that said they died under mysterious circumstances. Unfortunately, I've misplaced the story, but it must have implied suicide. I can't imagine how else I would have jumped to that conclusion. Or maybe I've read too many paranormal stories and assumed the ghosts were the victims of some morally ambiguous tragedy. Or else…"

He stood and walked over to a desk on the other side of the room. He pushed papers around until he found what he was looking for. He picked up a sheaf of printouts. "Here we go. I knew I had also read it somewhere else. This is from Thomas Fledgeling Longwood's diary. He lived down the street from the Brill House."

"I remember."

Troy stood in the middle of the room. He adjusted his glasses and read aloud, "*I learned today of the deaths of Mr. Brill and Mr. Cutler. Mr. Brill's housekeeper had the misfortune of finding them, slain and left in the second-floor bedroom. The police are investigating, but it seems these men finally faced the great sin they were committing.* That's vague, but I must have taken it to mean that Longwood thought they killed themselves because they were gay." He skimmed the rest of the page. "It says here that someone Longwood talked to had heard that a gun was found in Cutler's hand, but Longwood wasn't sure if the information was from a reliable source."

"Okay," said Finn.

Troy put the printouts back on the desk and frowned. Perhaps the idea had been planted in his head, but he dismissed it because it didn't make sense for the ghosts to have made him think the wrong thing. More to the point, the ghosts seemed to be gaining power, especially in their ability to manipulate space and dreams. When Troy first learned about Brill's and Cutler's deaths, that wasn't the case. Besides, that hypothesis conflicted with the new evidence. "I think I drew the wrong conclusion. Look." He picked up the police report and handed it to Finn. "They found the derringer in Cutler's hand, but the trajectory of the bullet was not consistent with a bullet fired by himself at close range."

Troy watched Finn scan the report. "How could they have known that?"

"Forensic science had developed enough by this point that they knew a lot about bullet wounds. This is after the Civil War, remember, when medicine had to develop rapidly to keep up with the increasingly lethal firearms that were being developed." Troy sat back down on the couch. "Here's the thing, though. I did some digging. After I talked to you this afternoon, I called my NYPD contact back. He told me two things. First, this is technically a cold case. They never arrested anyone, never really found any suspects, never closed the case."

"Wow."

"That's all in the report. What's not in the report is that they stopped looking abruptly. My contact found a handwritten note in the file that basically indicates that the police found out from one of Brill's tenants that Brill and Cutler were…" He paused to flip through a notepad he'd left on the coffee table. "Ah, here we go. 'Filthy sodomites.' The detective decided not to pursue the investigation after that."

"Fantastic. So, if the detective stopped investigating, how do you propose we solve the mystery?"

"There is some evidence in the report." Troy reached over and pointed to the bottom of the page. "The detective's notes are still here. He thought at first it was someone who knew both men, who they trusted enough to allow into the house. They were killed in their bedroom, and there was no real sign of a struggle anywhere else in the house."

Finn looked down at the report.

Troy said, "I think the answer will be in the journals. I mean, obviously, they aren't going to say, 'Mr. Smith killed me,' or whatever, but I think we can put together a list of suspects."

Finn put the pages on the coffee table and leaned back on the couch. He wiped his face with his hands.

"Are you okay?" Troy asked.

Finn lowered his hands and looked at Troy. His eyes were rimmed with red. "Yeah, I'm just really tired."

"I feel bad for keeping you out late."

"No, don't. I chose to come over here."

"Do you want to stay here tonight?"

Finn looked at him, his eyes wide, alarm evident on his face. "Troy…"

"I'm not propositioning you. I'm…worried, I guess. If I send you back to Manhattan, you're going to pass out on the train. I have a big bed. I'll even sleep on the couch if it makes you more comfortable. And I can lend you some clothes in the morning or a clean shirt at least."

Finn yawned. "You don't have to…" He collapsed back on the couch. "Yeah, I'm wiped. I think I will take you up on your offer. But you don't have to sleep on the couch."

When Finn's head lolled back, Troy wondered if he'd have to carry him to bed. Instead he offered his hand. "Come here," he said.

Finn took the hand and let Troy help him up. Troy

led him to the bedroom, where he helped Finn strip to his underwear and then helped him slide under the covers.

Troy went back into the living room and put things away before brushing his teeth, returning to his room, and changing out of his clothes. Finn was dead to the world, snoring softly. Troy stood next to the bed and watched him sleep for a moment, wondering what had drained his energy like that.

* * *

Finn was only vaguely aware of what was going on around him. One minute, he was drifting off to sleep on Troy's couch; then he felt himself being lifted and escorted into the bedroom. When he hit the mattress, he looked up and saw that he was in an opulent four-poster bed. The sheets were soft cotton that had been washed to the point of near destruction, but the quilt pulled over his body seemed expensive, down-filled and clean, with a satiny throw tossed over the whole affair.

Finn had two thoughts: first, he wondered why he was so exhausted and then remembered working twelve-hour days for Loretta all week and not sleeping pretty much at all; and second, his greatest desire in that moment was to have Troy's arms wrapped around him, to press into that wide chest and all that body heat. Because he was cold. Why was it so cold?

"Troy?" he murmured.

"Shh. You have a fever." The voice that rang through the room was male but definitely not Troy's.

"I don't remember getting sick."

"I expect it happened when you were out in the rain a couple of days ago."

Finn didn't remember rain either, but he opted not to argue the point. Instead, he let his head sink into the pillow and looked up at the canopy over his head, wondering when it was that Troy had bought this monstrosity and replaced the simple mattress and box spring that had sat on the floor of his room when they'd had sex recently. Come to think of it, Finn thought, what happened to Troy's sheets with the pink stripes, or his cheap foam pillows, and wasn't he allergic to down?

Finn was halfway toward groaning out loud at the realization that he'd slipped from his real life when Theodore Cummings Brill came into his frame of vision. He sat on the edge of the bed.

"Here is some water," he said.

Finn took the proffered glass. The water wasn't cold, but it was thirst-quenching. He handed the glass back to Teddy and said, "I feel all right, just really tired."

"The fever is breaking, then, perhaps."

Teddy looked at Finn with some eagerness, a smile playing on his lips now that Finn/Wash was apparently out of the dark. He really was extraordinarily handsome if you went for that whole stocky, bearded bear look. That was not normally Finn's thing—he liked 'em muscular and clean-shaven, in point of fact—but Teddy's face was pleasant and his body solid and strong.

"Have you been taking care of me all this time?"

"What is the last thing you remember?"

"Sitting on the sofa."

"Yes. That was yesterday morning."

"I've been out of it for that long?" The weird thing about this dream was that, unlike in previous dreams, Finn seemed to have autonomy over the words that came out of his mouth. Finn's incredulity was genuine—no way could he have just missed more than twenty-four hours. He'd never been that sick.

Teddy said, "Are you hungry? I could have Mrs. Morrison bring you some soup."

"No, I…" Finn struggled to sit up. He looked around the room. It was familiar, but when he searched whatever part of Wash's brain he was inhabiting for some clue as to his whereabouts, he came up empty. "Where am I?"

Teddy ducked his head and blushed. "Oh, well, I…" He coughed. "You are in my room. You were so sick, I thought it inappropriate to make you climb to the fourth floor."

Finn looked around. He recognized now that he was in the Brill House's second-floor bedroom. "If I was here for two days, where did you sleep?"

Teddy stood. He turned a deep shade of red and took a step back. "I…"

Finn caught sight of a pillow and blanket draped over a chaise—*the* chaise, if Finn was not mistaken, though it looked new instead of battered—and looked back at Teddy. "You slept there? That must have been uncomfortable."

"You were delirious. I did not think I should leave you."

Finn was touched. "Thank you."

"'Tis nothing you would not have done for me."

"That's true." Finn felt suddenly daring. "You won't have to sleep there tonight. You should sleep in your own bed again."

"The doctor said you should stay abed for at least another day after the fever broke."

"Then we will sleep here together."

Teddy looked befuddled.

"I'm not feverish anymore," Finn pointed out. Then, even more daring, he patted the space on the bed next to him. "Come here."

Teddy sat on the edge of the bed. Finn needed him to know that he was welcome. He wanted Teddy to share his bed, but more than that, he wanted him to share his life. He reached over and touched Teddy's back. He moved closer, wrapping an arm around Teddy's waist and pressing his face into Teddy's side.

"Please come here," he said into Teddy's shirt. "I need you to be close to me."

He felt Teddy sigh. "Wash," he whispered.

"I know it is wrong, but it is what I need right now." As the words left Finn's mouth, he realized he wasn't in control anymore, that he'd become more of a passive observer again, watching the world through Wash's eyes as if he were watching a movie.

Teddy turned and looked down at Wash/Finn. "You have no idea how long I have waited for your need to overcome whatever it is you think is right and proper."

"Teddy."

Teddy's body language relaxed. He moved closer to Wash/Finn and laid a hand on the side of his face. "Tell me what there is in your heart. We are quite alone, and you can be honest with me."

Finn lay back on the pillow again and closed his eyes, working to conjure up whatever was in Wash's heart. It occurred to him that it might not be so different from what was in his own heart as regarded the man whom he could sense lying next to him in a bed in his own timeline, one who was muscular and clean-shaven and had put him to bed with such care. He took a deep breath and said, "I have this vision sometimes of us becoming old men together, sharing this house as equals instead of landlord and tenant. We would live together as a husband and wife might, although of course neither of us is wifely."

Teddy snorted a laugh.

Wash/Finn took his hand. "What is in my heart is that I love you deeply, not just as a friend but in all the ways that we are told are shameful and horrific, but I cannot change how I feel or who I am. If that makes me horrific, then so be it. I can no longer deny it."

Teddy smiled. "I love you too, in all those same ways. If we come to this together, I do not see how it can be wrong."

Teddy leaned down and wrapped Wash/Finn up in his arms. Finn was content to savor the sensation. But then things started shifting again.

He came awake gradually and found himself tangled up with Troy. Troy's chest pressed into Finn's back. He had thrown an arm around Finn's waist and nudged his left leg between both of Finn's. Troy's even breathing indicated he was asleep, and the cotton pressing into Finn's back indicated he was still clothed. Finn's right arm had gone pins and needles. He moved his arm to get circulation flowing again, and his movement woke up Troy. Kind of.

"Finn," he murmured, clutching Finn's side and pushing his bulky body into Finn's back. Finn could feel Troy's erection pressing into the back of his thigh. Then there was a sigh, and the even breathing resumed.

Finn wondered what that meant. He managed to roll over so that he could see Troy, who still seemed to be lost to the world, his eyes closed, his lips parted. "Am I starring in some pornographic dream?" he wondered aloud, touching Troy's face.

"Mmm," said Troy.

Troy's arms came more firmly around Finn, but it was hard to say if Troy was awake or not. It didn't matter, because Finn liked the feeling of being wrapped up in his arms. He pressed his face into Troy's shoulder and inhaled, smelling a mix of the clean scent of Troy's laundry detergent, his spicy cologne, and his salty sweat.

Was he hoping this would happen? When Troy had offered the use of his bed, Finn had mentally gone back and forth about accepting, wondering if it was a good idea, although his mind had flashed on the possibility of a late-night tryst. Of course, nothing was ever easy, and his feelings for Troy were complicated, which was precisely why it might have been wiser to make Troy sleep on the couch.

Too late now, Finn thought. Troy sleepily mumbled his name again, and then spouted some random nonsense. His hips made an unmistakable movement against Finn's thigh, however. Definitely an erotic dream. Finn ran a hand along the length of Troy's arm to see how he'd react. Troy seemed to become more amorous in his sleep, rocking his hips and pressing closer to Finn, and his lips pursed as if he were waiting for a kiss. So Finn kissed him.

Finn was surprised when Troy reacted, parting his lips. He tasted of toothpaste and sleep and Troy. Finn plunged his tongue in and was met with Troy's. Then Troy's hand cupped Finn's ass.

"Are you awake now?" Finn asked.

"Mm-hmm," said Troy. "Are you?"

"As awake as ever."

Troy grabbed Finn's hand and placed it on his groin. Finn felt how very hard and large Troy was. "You wanna?" Troy asked.

"With you? Always."

"Even when you're mad at me?"

"Especially when I'm mad at you." Finn kissed him again. "Can I tell you a secret?"

"Please do."

Finn whispered, "Fighting with you gets me really hot. I have no idea why."

"Remind me to pick fights with you more often." Troy ran a hand down Finn's chest. "By the way, you're pale and you have stupid hair."

"You like my hair."

Troy ran his fingers through Finn's hair. "I love your hair." He kissed Finn. "Um," he mumbled into Finn's mouth. "That paper you wrote on...the topic... I mean, it was so dumb, I can't..."

"Knock it off. I'm plenty hot right now."

"Mmm, good."

They kissed urgently, tongues tangling. Troy's mouth was hot, as was the skin under Finn's hand. He tugged on Troy's T-shirt, and they worked together to squirm out of their clothes, their lips parting only long enough to pull off Troy's shirt. When they were both naked, Troy pulled Finn into his arms and pressed his hips forward so that their cocks rubbed together.

Finn felt out of breath suddenly, wrapped up in Troy, feeling the texture and surface of Troy's cock against his own. He loved being pressed against all that male flesh, loved the way Troy's hands caressed his arms, his back.

"Should I get the lube?" Troy asked.

"No, just like this."

Finn kissed Troy, sucking Troy's lower lip between his teeth. Troy moaned and sighed and moved his hips against Finn's. Finn's body tingled everywhere but most especially where their cocks pushed against each other. He pumped against Troy and ran his hands through Troy's silky hair, over the contours of the muscles on his arms. He dug his fingers into Troy's back, tracing the lines formed by muscle and sinew, and he memorized everything, every sound, smell, and sensation, every muscle and hair.

"So good," Troy said. "So fucking good. I love your body. I love how you taste."

Finn moved his head and kissed Troy's neck. He licked patterns there. He ran his hands through Troy's hair and tugged this time, pulling a gasp out of Troy but then a groan of appreciation.

Finn knew he was about to lose his grip on everything. He was completely overwhelmed by Troy's sweaty, salty, spicy scent, by the friction of their cocks rubbing together, by the sounds Troy was making. Every time Troy groaned, it reverberated in his chest and vibrated against Finn. He groaned one more time and came, his cock pulsing against Finn's, hot liquid shooting between them.

Troy's face went ecstatic, his eyes rolling into the back of his head, and Finn thought there was maybe nothing sexier than Troy when he was coming. Then everything merged and combined like a slap in the face, and Finn came too, shooting long ropes over Troy's chest. The strength of the orgasm overtook him, and an intense heat spread through his body. He rode it out and found Troy's mouth with his own, wanting to keep their bodies merged somehow, wanting Troy to know how much all this meant without having to say it.

* * *

Afterward, Finn related the details of his dream. Troy listened and stroked Finn's hair, enjoying the texture of it against his fingers.

"I don't know if it means anything, but it felt… important," Finn said.

"Now I'm curious. I've got Brill's ledgers. I wonder if he stopped charging Cutler rent. I will look into that tomorrow."

Finn settled his head against Troy's chest. "What were you dreaming about when I woke you up?"

"Hmm?"

"You were having a steamy dream when I woke up. What was it?"

"You're going to laugh at me."

"I won't."

"Do you remember the apartment I had in grad school? The place on Spring Street right off the Bowery that used to be a flophouse?"

"Kind of."

Troy shifted his weight a little. He smelled Finn's hair, which still bore hints of strawberry-scented shampoo. Kind of an odd choice, Troy thought, but still pleasant. "The apartment was kind of a shithole, but I was curious about the building, and I'm a nerd, so I looked into it. It was a saloon of ill-repute during the Gilded Age, somewhat famous for being the place old whores went to die. After I read that, I was surprised that the building was still standing, although it was only barely doing that."

"Uh-huh. This is all fascinating, but you seem to be evading my question."

"I'm setting the scene, darling. I dreamed I was living there again, only it had regressed back to its more colorful days, and so the first floor, rather than being the empty storefront it was during most of my tenure in the building, was a bar again, full of drunk men and scantily clad women."

"Okay. Was it the drunk men or the scantily clad women who had you moaning in your sleep?"

"Did I really moan?"

Finn nodded.

"Well, anyway. Neither of those was really lighting me on fire, but *you* were there. We met near the back, and I mentioned that I was conveniently renting rooms upstairs, so you followed me up there and then fucked my brains out. Or, I should say, you were in the process of fucking my brains out when you woke me up."

"Nice. Good thing I was available to make you come in real life."

"Indeed. I also thought that a fortuitous turn of events."

Finn laughed. "I like your dream better than mine."

They lay together in comfortable silence for a long time. "I'll lend you something to wear tomorrow so you don't have to do the walk of shame in the clothes you wore yesterday."

"It's fine. You may not have noticed, but I kind of wear the same thing every day."

"I *did* notice. As it happens, I spend a lot of time staring at your body, and if your T-shirts didn't change color, I would be convinced that you only owned one set of clothes."

"Loretta doesn't care what I wear. I figured out how to dress without looking ridiculous. Why stray from what works?"

"You could just stay naked all the time. That would be good also."

"Yeah, but then I'd get cold."

Troy laughed. "True enough."

"Probably you're going to tell me I'm a bad gay for not being a clotheshorse, but seriously, I'm missing the fashion gene or something, because I go into a store and get overwhelmed."

"Hey, I don't care that you dress like a college student still. You're great in all the ways that matter."

"Uh, thanks."

Troy felt content, holding Finn, talking about stupid things. He felt Finn drifting off to sleep, felt his breathing change where their chests pressed together. He smiled to himself. As Finn started to snore, Troy felt the pull of sleep and closed his eyes. He drifted himself and dreamed of nothing.

Chapter 12

Troy met Finn at Joyce after Finn had called saying he'd found something really interesting in Cutler's journal. Finn hadn't changed clothes; he was still wearing the peach polo shirt Troy had loaned him—it was tight on Troy but a little loose on Finn, and not in a bad way, Troy thought—and clearly hadn't shaved or washed his hair.

"I don't think peach is a good color for me," Finn said as he sat down.

"What makes you say that?" asked Troy. He took a sip of his beer. "You look hot. Or maybe that's all of this." He gestured over his own chin to indicate that he was referring to the two days of beard growth on Finn's face. "I like it. You should keep it. Or forego shaving more often. I like scruffy Finn. A lot." He leered.

Finn leveled his gaze at Troy. "Loretta kept commenting on the shirt. She wanted to know why I had changed my wardrobe."

"That's a sign you've grown too predictable. Change looks good on you. I will lend you clothes more often and confiscate your razor."

"Right. Well, anyway. You should see this." He carefully pulled the envelope holding Cutler's journal out of his bag. He pulled out the journal, flipped to a page at which he'd inserted a bookmark, and handed the whole thing to Troy. "February seventeenth."

Troy read. "*I did not know. How could I have? My life is over.*"

"So he got some kind of threat," Troy said.

"No, I don't think so."

"Why else would he think his life was over?"

"I mean, I guess it could be a threat, but I have an alternate theory."

"Which is?"

Finn motioned for Troy to give him the book back. He took it, closed it, and set it on the table. "When did you lose your virginity?"

Troy furrowed his brow. He wondered what Finn was getting at but answered the question. "I was fifteen."

"Fifteen! You *are* a slut."

Troy rolled his eyes. "Why? How old were you?"

"Twenty!"

"Okay. But, in my defense, well… Picture the hottest guy in your high school. Bonus points if he's a senior on the football team." When Finn raised a skeptical eyebrow, Troy punched him playfully and added, "No, seriously, picture that guy."

Finn closed his eyes briefly. "Okay."

Curious, Troy said, "Tell me about him."

"His name was Shawn. He was a blond senior in my Latin class freshman year. That was the first bona fide crush I ever had on a guy, and I had it bad. I spent more time staring at him than I did learning Latin. The sad part is that I'm pretty sure he wouldn't have been able to pick me out of a lineup."

"Well, okay," Troy said. "That guy. Imagine that instead of dating the head cheerleader or whatever, that he's gay, and he wants you."

"No way," Finn said.

Troy laughed. "Mine was named Keith. I gave him a

blowjob in the locker room after gym class one day. We both got detention for skipping our next class. Totally worth it. I thought that's all it would be, but then he propositioned me for sex, so you know I was at his house after school with bells on."

"Okay."

"It all came crashing to a halt when his cheerleader beard found out, and he stopped talking to me."

"You're such a weirdo."

"What were we talking about?"

Finn laughed. "Oh," he said at length. "Sorry, I was momentarily paralyzed by the vision of you giving Shawn a blowjob in a locker room."

"And how did that go for you?"

"It was good." He coughed. "Anyway, I don't think Cutler was getting threatened at all. I think this journal entry represents the…consummation of his relationship with Brill."

That surprised Troy, but it made a certain sense too. "He got laid, in other words."

"To put it delicately."

"You're such a prude."

"Whatever. Anyway, if you're a man in 1875 who just had sex for the first time and with another man to boot, you're bound to freak out, right?"

"I'd be mildly concerned about getting stoned."

"Mildly?"

"I pride myself on being very mellow."

"Please. You're as mellow as an AC/DC concert." Finn signaled for the waitress. "Anyway, that's my theory.

In the next entry, he talks about some sort of arrangement he made with Brill in which part of his income goes to the household at large, but he no longer rents a room. I'm pretty sure that means he essentially moved into Brill's room."

"How delightfully progressive of them." Troy grinned. "I looked through Brill's ledgers this afternoon, and that would be consistent with what I found. He stops accounting for rent on Cutler's room and indeed seems to have rented it to somebody else in the spring of 1875, but there's a spot for 'Miscellaneous Income' that I'm going to assume is whatever Cutler's contribution was."

"Sure, that makes sense. Is there any mention of the arrangement in Brill's journals?"

"Not that I've come across yet."

"Because the thing is, the next few journal entries are largely about Cutler's worry that the other tenants would find out what was going on. He cooked up some lie about it being a money-saving arrangement, and most of the tenants probably knew that Brill and Cutler were close friends."

"I wonder if they could conceive of Brill and Cutler fucking. Today, we find out that two men are sharing a room, we assume they are sleeping together, but in Brill and Cutler's day, it wasn't that weird for two bachelors to share living arrangements like that."

"The tenants knew by the time Brill and Cutler died. That's how the police found out."

"Good point."

The waitress came. Troy ordered a second beer and some chicken wings.

"Gross," said Finn.

"I went to the gym before coming here. Allow me the

indulgence."

Finn rolled his eyes.

Troy said, "Remember that Rawley guy Brill ran into a few journals ago? Down at the fish docks?"

"Yeah."

Since they were sharing, Troy reached for his bag. From it, he pulled a large envelope and placed it on the table. "I did some searching. All I really had to go on was the name Rawley and his approximate age, but I think I found him. John Rawley was a mediocre artist in Brooklyn at this time. The KCHS has a few of his paintings on display at their main museum. Mostly, he painted watery landscapes. There are a bunch of these gigantic canvases depicting the Hudson that he painted when he lived upstate." Troy held his arms wide to demonstrate. "He also painted a series of landscapes in the early 1870s called 'Fish Docks,' though, so you can do the math. Most of these are in private collections, but the KCHS has one. I was underwhelmed." He pulled from the envelope some 8"x10" prints of the paintings and handed them to Finn.

Finn flipped through them. "Wow. These are breathtakingly boring."

"I thought, based on that one journal entry, that Rawley might have borne Brill some ill will, but I can't find anything to substantiate that. As far as I can tell, their paths never crossed again, although who knows? If they both lived in the same neighborhood and liked to hang out at the docks, they could have run into each other again and just not mentioned it."

A waitress came by and plopped a mug full of beer and a plate piled high with hot wings on the table. Finn raised an eyebrow when Troy brandished a wing and bit into it. Troy didn't care; hot wings were one of his vices, and he'd be damned if he let Finn judge him for it.

Finn said, "It's all about timing, I think. They had one encounter in the early 1870s. If Brill never mentioned Rawley again, they probably never ran into each other again. In the meantime, that's a lot of years to sit around waiting to kill someone."

Troy washed his chicken down with a big gulp of beer. "I agree. And that's even assuming this is the same Rawley. It could have been some other Rawley who didn't even live in Brooklyn." Troy put his mug down.

"Square one," said Finn.

"Yep. You want a wing?"

"No, thank you."

"You sure? Or you can order some other food. My treat."

"Nah, I'm okay. I had a late lunch."

Troy ate silently and watched Finn, who had turned sideways in his chair and was looking around the room. He nursed a beer and seemed to be lost in his own thoughts. Troy took a moment to admire his profile. It occurred to him that he should probably mention some other research ideas he'd had. It seemed wrong to go down other avenues without at least consulting Finn first. "Would you be horribly offended if I brought in some outside people to help us?"

Finn turned back. "Why would I be offended?"

"I don't know. I'd sort of come to think of this as *our* project. I wouldn't bring in anyone else except that I think we need some minds with expertise you and I don't have."

"Uh, okay. Like forensic people?"

"Among others." Troy figured Finn would mock him

for at least one of the people he had in mind, so he didn't elaborate.

"Sure, it's fine."

"Great, because I have a crazy idea for your next day off."

Finn frowned. "I'm not going to like it, am I?"

Chapter 13

"This is nuts," Finn said from behind Troy as they walked from the subway. "What the hell neighborhood is this, anyway?"

"Don't worry, we're still in Brooklyn. Welcome to Victorian Flatbush. Although, if anyone asks, this is Ditmas Park and before you tell me it's a shithole neighborhood, may I point out that the houses lining the sidewalks here are multimillion-dollar homes."

Troy loved this neighborhood. As he and Finn walked along Albemarle Road, he looked at the old Tudor-style houses. While in grad school, he'd had a job as a guide for the Victorian Flatbush House Tours, so he knew a lot about who had lived in which houses, when they had been constructed, and what the architectural details meant. Most of the homes had been built in the 1890s and were beautifully maintained. Troy always thought walking through this part of Brooklyn was a little like taking a trip back in time.

"It almost doesn't look like Brooklyn," Finn said.

They were on their way to speak with an honest-to-God spiritualist, a woman Troy had found through a group of Civil War reenactors he knew. She billed herself as being a spiritualist of the Victorian mold, and made money conducting séances and speaking to the dead. Finn had made it quite clear he thought this was bunk, but Troy thought it was worth it to speak to the woman and see if she could offer any guidance. Maybe she was a fraud, but Troy figured it was no skin off his nose. She was seeing them as a favor. He figured it would be an interesting experience at least.

Besides, now that he knew ghosts were real, all sorts of

things that had once seemed ridiculous now seemed possible. And Finn had come with him, despite all the protesting.

He pulled from his pocket the piece of paper on which he'd written Maura Higham's address. He found the house easily enough. Finn still trailed behind, his head down as if he were lost in his own thoughts. It occurred to Troy that this was maybe how he liked Finn best, when he was quiet and thoughtful and not so angry, when he was working out some puzzle in his head. Not that he didn't enjoy a good verbal spar, just that the anger was getting tiring

Finn followed Troy up the stoop to the front door. Troy hit the buzzer. They were greeted by a slight woman in her fifties who looked to Troy a little like a cartoon witch.

"Ms. Higham?" Troy said.

"Yes."

"I'm Troy Rafferty, and this is Christopher Finnegan. I called about the ghosts at the Brill House?"

"Yes, of course. Come in. And call me Maura."

Maura led them to a parlor that looked like it had fallen right out of the mid-nineteenth century. She invited Troy and Finn to sit on a grandiose sofa upholstered in shiny blue brocade. When everyone was settled into a comfortable seat with a cup of tea, Maura said, "Now tell me about your ghosts."

Troy explained about the cold spots in the Brill House. Finn interrupted to quietly recount his occasional brief bouts of nausea. Troy jumped back in and explained about books flying off shelves. Then he glanced at Finn and said, "And there's one more thing."

Finn frowned. "Troy…"

"Maura should have an accurate picture of what's

been happening."

Finn rubbed his forehead. To Maura, he said, "Look, Troy's research indicates that the ghosts are probably two men who died in the house in 1878, a Mr. Brill and a Mr. Cutler. We've learned from their journals that the men were engaged in a homosexual relationship with each other."

"How did they die?"

"That's not entirely clear to us yet," said Troy. "I mean, they were both shot. Whether it was murder or suicide or both, we're not sure. The detective who investigated thought murder until he found out they were gay, at which point he dropped the investigation. Finn and I think the evidence gathered so far indicates murder. We're hoping the journals will have more clues. The last few volumes of Brill's journal are still at the KCHS's lab, but I intend to go through them when I get them back." Troy looked back at Finn, who was probably wondering the same thing Troy was. So Troy asked. "I hope you don't... I mean, you're not put off by our gay ghosts, are you?"

Maura laughed. "What? No, of course not."

"That's good, because here's another wrinkle." Troy took a deep breath. "Finn and I have both been having dreams. They seem to correspond with whose journal we're reading. I've been reading Brill's journals and usually see the world from Brill's perspective in the dreams. Likewise Finn with Cutler."

"What do you mean, 'see the world'?"

"It's like I'm reliving his life," Troy said. "I have no better way to explain it."

Maura nodded. She cupped her chin in her hand and looked down for a long moment. She looked up again and smiled. "An object like a journal can be a vessel for the soul.

The ghosts themselves are trapped in the house, but they could have embedded a part of themselves in the journals, so that they can reach you when you have the books with you."

Finn opened his mouth. Troy put a hand on his knee to shut him up.

"What is the nature of these dreams?" asked Maura.

"Sometimes they are just mundane things," said Troy. "Day-in-the-life kind of dreams. Finn had one where Brill and Cutler went shopping together. I had one where they took a walk through the neighborhood."

Maura nodded. "What else?"

Troy glanced at Finn again. "Finn may disagree with me, but sometimes the dreams seem to show events not recounted in the journals. Things more personal. A conversation between Brill and Cutler, for instance, some important stepping stone on their way to falling in love with each other."

"It's nonsense," said Finn. "I mean, we're having the dreams because we're reading the journals and our minds are filling in the details."

Maura reached over and patted Finn's shoulder. Finn winced. She then turned to Troy. "Anything else?"

"Well…"

"Troy, don't."

"I think it's relevant." Troy looked at Maura. "The dreams are sometimes of an…erotic nature."

Finn grunted. Maura sat back and scratched her chin.

"What do you feel in these dreams?" she asked.

Finn shook his head. To Troy, he said quietly, "She sounds like a shrink."

"Will you calm down?" To Maura, Troy said, "I think I feel whatever Brill was feeling. If he's frightened or happy or aroused, I feel that. And love too. When I'm Brill in the dream and I'm with Cutler, I feel love for him."

Maura lowered her head for a moment. "And you, Mr. Finnegan?"

Finn crossed his arms over his chest. Troy expected him to deny it, but after a pause, he nodded.

"I've seen this kind of thing before," Maura said. "I think the ghosts want you to understand their circumstances, to know what it was like for them."

"If Brill and Cutler are even our ghosts," Finn said.

Maura shrugged. "I guess you can't be certain, but Mr. Rafferty seems pretty convinced."

"The evidence seems conclusive." Troy leaned closer to Maura. "Pardon my colleague's skepticism. You should have seen how long it took me to convince him there were any ghosts at all. He still barely believes it."

Maura smiled knowingly. "Do you have any documentation on sightings at the house prior to when you took over curating it?"

"Yes. Most of it's standard, I think. Reports of cold spots and strange noises. There are letters and things passed down from previous owners. The Brill House is actually in a book about haunted properties in Brooklyn that was published fifteen or so years ago."

Maura tilted her head. "No previous reports of the ghosts manifesting themselves?"

"What do you mean?"

"Have apparitions of the ghosts ever been seen? Or have there been reports of objects moving, doors slamming when no one is near them, that sort of thing?"

"None that I've come across," said Troy, "but I'm not sure that's a reason to believe these things have never happened."

"Is it possible that activity has escalated?"

"Sure. I mean, the books flying off the shelves is a new phenomenon, as far as I know. I've certainly not seen any descriptions of incidents like that in the house." Troy turned to Finn. "And then there's the chaise longue thing."

Finn shook his head. "I don't want to—"

"I think the ghosts steered us toward Cutler's journal."

"How do you mean?" asked Finn.

Troy hesitated. "You said it yourself, Finn. Something really wanted you to, um, get to the chaise."

Finn rolled his eyes. "Yeah, I really wanted it."

"But you told me you were surprised by how much you wanted it," Troy said. "I think that could be a manifestation of something. The ghosts planting the idea in your head, maybe."

Finn sat back and didn't say anything.

"Finn talked me into sitting on this chaise in the parlor at the Brill House," Troy said. "I felt something strange, and when I investigated, I found that Cutler's journal had been sewn into the upholstery."

Maura looked surprised. "What made you want to get Troy to sit on the chaise?" she asked Finn.

Finn moved his hands around. "I just felt that I had to… I mean, I…"

"It was my raw animal magnetism," Troy said.

Finn looked mortified, his face flushed. He squirmed

in his chair. "Look, I…"

"You desired Troy," Maura said.

"Yeah."

"Is that unusual? For you to desire a man?"

"No, I'm gay. But——"

"You also, Troy?"

"Yes, but——"

Maura waved her hand. "It would be too much for these ghosts to make you desire something you would never want but if they could take something subconscious and bring it to the fore, they could use your desires for their own ends."

Something about that made Troy uneasy, but he decided the silver lining was that the ghosts wouldn't have been able to make either of them feel something they hadn't felt before.

"I didn't desire Troy before then," said Finn.

"Oh, please," Troy said. "That's a terrible lie."

Finn threw his hands up in the air. "Can we not analyze it? I don't care to dissect my sex life right now. How about we just talk about the fucking ghosts so that we can call it a day, and I can go back to my job that actually pays me instead of running all over Brooklyn trying to solve the mystery of the gay Victorian ghosts haunting the Brill House."

"Okay." Troy put up his hands to demonstrate he was backing off.

"I think what's happening here is that the ghosts are exploiting something that already existed between you to achieve their own goal," said Maura. "I assume they are trying to help you solve their murder. They aren't strong enough to manifest themselves as physical apparitions, and there's a limit to how much they can manipulate physical objects, but it appears they can get in your heads and steer you toward clues."

"Yes, that is what I assumed," said Troy.

"This is nonsense," said Finn.

"Often, spirits will linger in order to convey something to people who visit the property they inhabit. Have they tried to send you a specific message?"

"Other than, 'We're here, we're queer'?" Troy said. "Not as far as I can tell. They seem to want us to know what their lives were like, which is why, I assume, they steered us toward Cutler's journal. Other than that, your guess is as good as mine."

"It's worth thinking about. Next time you have an experience involving them, consider what they might be trying to say."

Troy saw the wisdom in Maura's advice, though Finn continued to grumble about not believing any of it. Troy and Maura talked for another ten minutes, mostly speculating based on the evidence Troy had seen to that point. They wrapped up their discussion, and Maura said she'd take some time to think on it more, and then she led them to the door.

Once he and Finn were outside, Troy said, "You could have tried to be polite. I know you're not actually this stubborn."

"Did you have to tell her about what's going on with us?"

"Is it a secret?"

"I guess not." Finn stomped ahead a few steps, then spun around and looked at Troy. "Maybe I just don't think everyone needs to know our business. We just met the woman."

"I'm sorry, I thought it was relevant."

Finn's nostrils flared. "You know what *is* relevant? The fact that everything happening between us could be because of these fucking ghosts, and everything I feel now or have felt over the last few weeks could be bullshit."

"I don't really think that's the whole truth."

"You believe this woman, though, don't you? She said they're manipulating us. They planted the idea in my head that I desired you, so that I'd steer you to the journal."

"That's really not quite what she said. You're twisting it around. She said the ghosts were manipulating desires we already had. Which may or may not be true, I don't know. Besides, I thought you thought all of this was bullshit."

"I don't know what to think anymore." Finn rubbed his forehead. "I have to get back to Loretta. I'm supposed to be transcribing her notes this afternoon. I've already taken too long a lunch break, so now I'll have to work late."

"I'm sorry."

Finn waved his hand. "Let's just… I'm going back to the city. You taking the train?" He turned around again and walked back toward the subway.

"Yeah. I'm coming."

Chapter 14

When Finn went to the Brill House the following Monday, Troy opened the door looking out of sorts. His dark hair—rarely ever out of place—was damp and disheveled, and he was frowning, making the lines on his face more pronounced than they usually were.

"Is everything okay?"

Troy moved out of the way to let him in. After he closed the door, he led Finn to his office. "I finished my work early, so I decided to kill time by going to the gym."

"Ah, say no more. The decision to go to the gym never ends well for me either."

"Ha." Troy walked into his office and dropped into his chair. "Everything was fine until I was changing in the locker room afterward. Then this guy comes in. I've seen him before. We used to work out at the same time when I worked at the main building of the KCHS. And, I swear, I've never said one word to this guy before. But he walks right up to me and goes, 'Stop staring at my ass, faggot.' And, I mean, what the hell would make him do that? First of all, his ass is *not* interesting enough to stare at, and second, I had just been bench pressing twice his body weight."

Finn sat down. "How did he know you're gay?"

Troy shrugged. "I will admit to occasionally flirting with guys at the gym. And it's possible I was wearing a T-shirt from a charity bike race I did last year that had some rainbows on it. I cut the sleeves off, of course, to show off the guns." He flexed, but it was clear to Finn that his heart wasn't really in it. Troy lowered his arms. "I don't know, it's not like it's a secret, and you know that I sort of make a habit of not keeping it a secret. I live in New York! The whole reason I came here for college is that it's like Mecca for gay men. Sure, my gym is in Brooklyn and not Chelsea, but I've never been harassed there before."

"Did this guy do anything to you besides call you names?"

"He shoved me into a locker. Then I grabbed him by the front of his T-shirt and said something incendiary. Then he called me a cocksucker but backed off. I showered quickly and got out of there." Troy rubbed his forehead. "I feel like such a coward. Why didn't I punch that guy in the face?"

"Because *he* harassed *you*? Because, despite the fact that you're this big, beefy guy, you're actually nice and nonviolent?"

Troy propped his elbow on the desk and rested his chin in his hand. "Because despite all the years of progress, we're still discriminated against but are trained to sit back and take it?"

"I didn't say that."

"That's how I feel sometimes."

Finn wondered how much of Troy's gym habit could be attributed to aesthetics, as he claimed. "Is that why you've bulked up so much?"

Troy looked down at his lap. "I think there's some essential part of my nature that will always be that boy who got picked on in school for being too much like a girl." He looked up. "I know I can't change who I am, but I do have control over some things, and my body is one of those things."

Finn couldn't think of a time he'd ever seen Troy this vulnerable, and still there was a lot he wasn't saying. Finn got up, walked around the desk, and stood next to Troy. He stroked Troy's hair, tried to smooth it down to the way it should have been. Troy responded by leaning toward Finn and pressing his face into Finn's stomach. He wrapped his arms around Finn's waist. They stayed like that for a long time, Troy hugging Finn, Finn smoothing down Troy's hair. Finn thought Troy might have been crying—and that was something he felt completely unable to deal with—but when Troy looked up, his eyes were dry.

"Thank you," Troy said.

"Of course." Finn wasn't sure what he'd done, but he was happy it helped. "It's not like I'm not familiar with what you're going through. I was an outcast in school but mostly because I was nerdy. Things turned around for me when I came out, actually. Being gay gave me some cachet among my peers. Gay people in the media are never nerds. You ever notice that? They're always cool and fashionable."

Troy fingered his glasses. "You're a weird one, Christopher Finnegan. I can't believe you would parlay your sexuality to win cool points."

"It didn't work that well. As you know, I can barely dress myself. The girls caught on pretty quickly that I was useless as a shopping buddy. But for, like, two weeks in high school, I was the coolest."

"Well, I think you're pretty cool." Troy smirked, then reached over and took Finn's hand.

"That's cheesy." Finn intertwined his fingers with Troy's. "I like Clark Kent better."

"Huh?"

Finn looked down at Troy. "You have kind of a Superman quality. I mean, by all outward appearances, you're perfect. You're handsome. You have a perfect body.

You're smart and successful. Everybody wants you. You could probably do anything you set your mind to. Superman. It's intimidating. But sometimes you put on the glasses and become more like Clark Kent. He's dorky and bumbles things. He can't get a date with the person he wants most. He's flawed. I like you better when you're more like Clark Kent."

Troy narrowed his eyes. "So you think I should stumble around more? That I should be more of a failure?"

"No, not at all. The only real difference between Superman and Clark Kent is a pair of horn-rimmed glasses, right?" Finn tapped the side of Troy's glasses. "He still has the superpowers but he's more…down-to-earth as Clark, I guess. More relatable." He leaned down and whispered in Troy's ear, "That, and I think a nice pair of glasses on a good-looking guy is sexy as hell."

Troy laughed. He reached up and ran a finger along Finn's jaw. "I see you took my advice and started shaving less frequently."

"It could be that I don't have time to shave every day."

"It could be that you want me to find you attractive. Which I do. A lot."

Troy closed the space between them and kissed Finn. Finn put a hand on Troy's shoulder to keep from toppling over, and he could feel the tension there. Somewhere midkiss, the tension started to ease. Finn found he wanted to take away Troy's stress. And what did that say about their relationship now?

He eased away and stood up straight again. He wondered what had come over him. Hadn't he just been yelling at Troy a few days ago? When had he gone all mushy? He thought about the ghosts, imagined they were hovering around him then, making him like Troy for their own ends. He wasn't sure what was going on, but a subject change seemed a good course of action.

Troy seemed to feel the same way. As Finn retreated to his chair, Troy said, "So did you learn anything interesting since the last time I saw you?"

"A lot of this is more of the same." Finn pulled Cutler's journal from his bag. "There are long stretches where he has nothing to say; then every now and then, he has some insight about Brill that even I will admit is a little bit adorable—"

"Show me an example."

Finn smiled. He had one in mind. He flipped through the journal until he found the entry he was looking for. He read aloud, "*Today I noticed that Teddy has a scar right near the hairline on his forehead. I can't believe I never noticed before. I thought I had every part of Teddy's body memorized.*" Finn looked up and raised an eyebrow. "I think that's not an exaggeration."

Troy chuckled.

"*When I asked about it, he said it was from a scuffle he had with his brother when they were children. The reason I had not noticed it was that he often wears his hair so as to cover it, but this time, the wind had gotten the better of him. I asked why he was ashamed. After all, scars are evidence of a body lived in, of experience, of age. Teddy stammered but did not otherwise have an answer for me.*"

"Okay, that is adorable," said Troy.

"Anyway, I'm up to the early part of 1876 and have no insights into the murder."

Troy nodded. "I don't know if this is relevant, but toward the end of 1875, Brill started writing about some kid he used to see around the fish docks. He mentions going to the docks much less often after he and Cutler began their relationship. Still, my suspicion was that there was something about the fishermen he found appealing, and let's face it, burly men hauling in large nets full of fish?"

Finn nodded to acknowledge the point.

"Anyway, in the fall of 1875, he befriended a boy who has thus far gone nameless. Brill calls him simply 'the boy.' I've gathered that this boy was fourteen or fifteen, and he worked as a day laborer or something at the fish market. Brill's affection seems fatherly, I would guess borne of the fact that he knew he'd never be able to have children. This seems to be an empty hole in his life. I think he really wanted kids."

"Okay."

"My gut tells me this is important, so I hope to come up with the boy's identity soon."

Finn agreed that, at minimum, this was an interesting development. "You think the kid killed Brill and Cutler?"

"I honestly have no idea. I wouldn't be able to tell at this point because Brill just adores this kid, so he might not notice if the kid did something menacing. It just feels important. Has Cutler mentioned him?"

"I don't remember any mention of a teenage boy. I'll go back and look."

Troy looked at his desk. He rubbed his forehead.

"You want to ditch this for tonight?" Finn asked.

"I'm just tired."

"You should go home and go to bed."

"You're probably right." Troy didn't make any move to pack up his stuff, though.

"I'll go with you, if you want."

Troy looked up. "I do want that, yes."

"Then let's go."

* * *

Troy couldn't get over how *nice* Finn was being and wondered how much of it was genuine affection or if it was sympathy over the gym attack. Not that it mattered, since Troy was getting what he wanted, namely Finn all hot and bothered in his bed. They were kissing, Finn kneeling on the bed, Troy standing next to it. Troy very much enjoyed the rough scratch of Finn's chin against his own, the stubble there reminding Troy that this was a man he was kissing, a man he craved.

Troy pulled Finn's shirt off, and once Finn's hands were free, he set to unbuttoning Troy's shirt while nibbling on his jaw. Troy's body seemed to strain toward Finn's, and he couldn't keep his hands away. He ran his palms over Finn's shoulders, his chest, his arms.

Finn kissed Troy's mouth again as he peeled away Troy's shirt. Finn pulled off his undershirt too, and then dug fingers into his shoulders. Troy hissed with the unexpected pain of that.

"You okay?" Finn asked.

"I guess I hit that locker harder than I thought."

Finn put his hands on Troy's shoulders and turned him around. Troy felt Finn's hot breath on the back of his neck. Finn's fingers lightly trailed over the most painful part of Troy's back. "This is a hell of a bruise. It's sort of purple."

"Really?"

"Yeah. It didn't hurt?"

"Not really. Not until you poked at it."

"I'm sorry. I'll make it better."

Finn's lips skimmed over his skin, first just fluttering over the bruised area, light as a feather, then a little more forceful, planting kisses along the width of Troy's back. Troy couldn't deny that it felt good, but his heart sank a little as he realized that all this attention probably was out of pity or sympathy. Troy didn't want Finn's sympathy. His desire, his affection, yes, but he didn't want to be pitied.

As Finn's lips pressed into his back, though, Finn's hands moved around his sides and slid up his chest. Finn's erection pressed into the crack of Troy's still-clothed ass. Needing suddenly to feel more of Finn's hot flesh pressed against his own, he moved Finn's hands down to the clasp of his pants. Finn undid the button and then slid down the zipper. He reached a hand into Troy's underwear and wrapped his fingers around Troy's hard cock.

"Does your back feel better now, baby?" Finn murmured against Troy's shoulder.

Troy threw his head back, succumbing to the pleasure as Finn's hand started to move up and down the length of his cock. "Yeah," he managed to get out. "Good as new."

"Good," Finn said. "Because I want you on it."

Troy moaned in response. He turned around and put his hands on either side of Finn's face before pulling him in for a kiss. He opened his mouth to let Finn in, and Finn took the invitation, thrusting his tongue inside Troy's mouth. Troy pushed his own pants down his legs, stood back up, and undid the button on Finn's jeans. Finn wriggled out of them, then pressed the length of his body against Troy's. Finn's cock pressed against Troy's, and Troy groaned at the friction, their skin pressing together making him forget to think, his desire for Finn becoming a blind need.

Finn thrust his fingers into Troy's hair and pulled him close. They kissed again. Troy loved kissing Finn, loved the taste of his mouth, the way their lips fit together, the little sounds Finn made. Finn moved his hips against Troy's, driving their cocks together, and Troy started to feel as he always did with Finn, as if his skin were screaming, as if he were about to fly to pieces.

Finn put his hands on Troy's shoulders and pulled, knocking Troy onto the bed on his stomach. He rolled over, and Finn straddled him. Finn's curly hair was disheveled, and his skin was flush. Troy ran his hands over the rough fuzz of Finn's chest hair. He slid his fingers along the line of Finn's jaw, liking the sensation of Finn's rough stubble against his hands. Then he pulled Finn down for another kiss.

Finn managed to get a hand between them. He stroked both of their cocks together and grunted. Troy slid his tongue into Finn's mouth. He loved the pressure of Finn's big hands against his cock, the texture of their bodies moving together. Finn moved away slightly and slid his hand over Troy's balls, then around to his entrance.

"Gonna come too soon," Finn said. "Want to fuck you."

"No one's stopping you." Troy spread his legs.

Finn had a condom and lube out of the bedside drawer in record time. Then he dove, pressing his face against Troy's groin. Finn licked his balls and then moved lower. Troy felt Finn's tongue at his hole and tangled his fingers in Finn's hair, grinding against Finn's face. Finn was propped up mostly on his knees and Troy's body. He ripped the wrapper off the condom, and then rolled it on. It was an interesting bit of magic, how quick and flexible Finn proved to be, but Troy didn't have time to wonder at Finn's flexibility, because then

Finn's mouth was on the move again, and he was pressing a lubed-up finger into Troy.

Finn didn't waste a lot of time with preparation. He stretched Troy and asked if it felt okay, and Troy could only nod, welcoming the pain if only Finn would just hurry up, wanting so badly to get fucked, to feel Finn's body against his. Finally, *finally*, Finn licked a long trail up the middle of Troy's chest. Finn's lips then covered Troy's, and Troy gasped as he felt the head of Finn's cock pressing into him.

"Jesus," Troy said on an exhale.

"Do you always see the Lord during sex?"

"Only with you. Fuck me."

Finn grunted and started to move. Troy's body gave way, the searing pain of initial penetration easing into something far more pleasurable. He adjusted his hips to get a better angle. The head of Finn's cock pressed against his prostate, sending pulses and sparks to every corner of his body. "Oh, that's the spot,"

"It feels so good inside you." Finn's face contorted in pleasure. "So hot and tight."

Troy wanted to respond, but he'd lost the ability to form words and instead muttered incoherently as he felt his orgasm building. His skin was on fire everywhere it touched Finn. He put his hand between them and stroked his own cock until he was hovering just at the edge of the cliff, everything heat and electricity in the places where his and Finn's bodies were joined. Finn slapped Troy's hand out of the way and started pulling on his cock.

"Come for me, Troy,"

"I'm almost there. Kiss me."

Finn bent down, and their lips met again. Finn's

mouth was hot and metallic and so wonderful. Troy curled his tongue against Finn's and put his hands on Finn's back. Finn's thumb slid over the head of his cock. Finn pressed into the spot just under the head like he knew that was the detonation button, and then everything exploded. Troy shut his eyes as he came, his whole body screaming with intensity of the orgasm, and he shook as he shot all over his own chest.

When he looked up, Finn was gazing at him with wide eyes. He thrust into Troy a few more times, then murmured, "So good," and then his body vibrated as he came on a long moan that sounded like "Troy" but could have been nonsense.

* * *

Later, they lay in bed together, Finn's leg thrown over Troy, Troy's fingers idly combing through Finn's hair. Finn liked the sensation of that, of Troy's fingers softly scraping along his skull. He put a hand on Troy's chest and felt content.

"So I've been reading this book on sexual practices in the early part of the twentieth century," Troy said.

"For tips?"

Troy's chest rumbled with soft laughter. "Did you know that before World War II, many men considered only the bottom to be a fairy?"

"Does that mean that you're gay but I'm not?"

"Perhaps in the eyes of some. Homosexuality was not condemned as vehemently in the 1920s and '30s as it would be later. Some gay GIs in Europe during World War II were surprised to find that southern Italy was super gay. The Catholic church spent so much energy condemning sexual relations between men and women before marriage that many rationalized sex between men as not that bad and, more to the point, you weren't really sinning if you were the one doing the penetrating because that was still considered a masculine thing to do. It was when you bottomed that things got a little problematic. Men willing to do that were considered less than men, or as some kind of third sex."

"Interesting." Finn yawned and pressed himself against Troy. He was satisfied when Troy's arms came around him. "For the record, I think you are most definitely a man. It's one of the few things I like about you."

"Thanks, I think. You ever bottom, Finn?"

"Rarely. I mean, I have a few times and, I don't know, it felt weird to me."

"Maybe you just had the wrong partner."

"Maybe."

"Of course, as an avowed bottom, I do not have a problem with you wanting to top all the time. For the record."

Finn chuckled and pressed his face into Troy's shoulder. "So noted."

"I'm just pointing out how compatible we are."

Finn sighed. This conversation was starting to veer a little toward a place that Finn wasn't willing to go, namely a conversation about feelings. "Yeah, yeah."

"I don't know if you noticed, but we've actually been getting along all day."

Finn *had* noticed that he was feeling much less animosity toward Troy than usual. In fact, what he was feeling now was a lot of affection. And how weird was that? "Do you have a point?"

"You like me," Troy said. He sounded smug.

"A tiny bit." It was true that Finn was starting to develop

feelings for Troy—strange happy feelings, deep emotional feelings, feelings that made him think it was better to linger in bed with Troy after sex rather than to run out the door—but he didn't want to give Troy the satisfaction of admitting that. "It's not worth gloating about."

Troy laughed. "You're a stubborn bastard, baby."

Chapter 15

Troy was buzzed into Finn's building. As he climbed the stairs, he wondered at the history of the place; it looked like a former tenement. When he got upstairs, he knocked on the apartment door and was greeted by Janice, who grinned widely.

"Hello, Troy."

"Hi, Janice. Is Finn home? I'm hoping yes. If you buzzed me in so that you could have your wild way with me, I'm sad to say that not only are you not my type, but I'm quite smitten with your roommate. No offense."

Janice let him in. As she closed the door, she said, "The sad thing is that it would not be the first time a man came over to see me and wound up sleeping with Finn."

"Really?"

She led him into the living room. It had been a while since Troy had been to the apartment, and he hadn't remembered it looking quite so homey. Troy's space was always disheveled and cluttered, but Finn's place was neat—by Janice's preference or Finn's, Troy wasn't sure—but a little worn around the edges, so everything looked comfortable and lived in, from the threadbare beige sofa to the secondhand tables to the orange crocheted throw tossed over a chair in the corner.

"That's an important lesson," said Janice. "Don't ever let your closeted boyfriend meet your gay roommate."

"Words to live by. Although at least you knew you were dating a closet case then. Maybe Finn did the world a favor."

"He was really hot, though. I had hoped to sleep with him at least once, but the first night I dragged him home, he took one look at Finn, and I became invisible."

"That's understandable. Not that you aren't a lovely woman, just that Finn is, well…"

"I know," said Janice. "You are looking quite dashing, by the way. I figured you should know, in case Finn hasn't told you."

"Why, thank you. And he has, just not in so many words."

"That's good. I worried he was expending all of his energy talking about you with me." She lowered her voice. "He'd kill me if I told you this, but the tone has changed somewhat lately. At first, it was mostly, 'Troy makes me so mad, he's so annoying,' and so on, but lately, it's all, 'Troy said this the other day, Troy did that,' not even angry."

"Progress."

"I'd say so. And I'm glad for it. He's been lonely a lot lately, I think. This job with Loretta Kitteredge is chewing up so much of his time, and he's under a lot of pressure to do well. Well, and she's insane. Calls in the middle of the night, makes him work late, acts as though a book about a woman who's been dead for ninety years is a matter of life and death."

"I know."

Janice hugged him, which came as a surprise. Troy hugged her back.

"You're good for him," she said as she pulled away. "Anyway. Don't tell him I said anything. He's in his room."

Troy went down the hall. He knocked on Finn's door, and when there was no answer, he opened it. He saw Finn asleep on his back on the bed, his mouth agape, Cutler's journal open beside him.

Troy closed the door gently. He walked over to the bed and sat on the edge of it. Finn looked untroubled in his sleep. Troy wished Finn looked this relaxed more often. He wanted to take some of the stress from Finn's life. There was no denying it anymore. He had fallen for Finn hard. Would that horrify Finn or charm him?

Only time would tell, Troy figured. He hated to wake Finn, but he ran a hand down the side of Finn's face. Finn sighed in his sleep and leaned into Troy's hand. He came awake slowly and wrapped a hand around Troy's wrist. He murmured something nonsensical as his eyes fluttered open.

"Hi," said Troy.

Finn smiled. "Hi. I'm dreaming."

"Nope. Your dream has come true. I am actually here in the flesh."

"That's good. I love you, Troy." Then he was asleep again.

That stunned Troy. He stared at Finn for a long time, trying to process his sleepy words, wondering if they could possibly be true, hoping they were. He looked over Finn, from his curly blond hair to the scruffy beard growth on his chin to his rumpled T-shirt and shorts, right down to his neatly trimmed toenails. They'd known each other for more almost fifteen years, and they'd argued and agreed and made love, and Troy could not imagine a person he'd rather do all those things with. The truth was that he'd probably been in love with Finn for a long time. It was why he'd asked Finn to help him with this mystery, wasn't it? What other reason was there?

Troy leaned down and kissed Finn's forehead. "I love you too."

Finn stirred. "What was that?"

"Nothing. Are you awake now?"

"Eh." Finn stretched, throwing his arms over his head and flexing his feet, his long body displayed all along the length of the bed. "What are you doing here?"

"I wanted to see you, I guess. Also, I found something interesting in Brill's journal today. Janice let me in."

Finn moved over on the bed and patted the mattress next to him. Troy pulled some photocopied pages out of his pocket, and then lay down next to him. "I've got the name of the boy Brill was looking after."

"Oh?"

"Samuel Redding."

Finn yawned. "Should I know that name?"

Troy unfolded the pages and handed them to Finn. "Don't know. He was a teenager in the 1870s, working down at the fish docks in Brooklyn. He went on to own his own fishing boat and eventually a distribution company that delivered fresh fish to a number of high-end restaurants in the city. So not famous as such, except in certain circles, but definitely successful."

Finn sat up. "Okay."

"Brill took him under his wing, basically. Sam Redding was orphaned when he was twelve or thirteen and so was sort of at loose ends, picking up odd jobs. Brill started paying him to do things like shovel snow and clean up leaves. Eventually Brill hired a tutor and paid for Sam's education. He let the kid sleep at the house when he had nowhere else to go."

"That's interesting," said Finn as he scanned the pages. "How does this tie into the mystery?"

"Don't know."

"Was this Redding kid also gay?"

"No, I don't think so. Records indicate he married a woman in 1888 and had six kids over the course of ten years."

"They were busy."

"Yeah. It's frustrating that I don't have the volume after this one back yet, because I'd love to know how Sam Redding factors into the rest of the story here, or if he does. Maybe it's not relevant at all. But I like the idea of Brill having a protégé."

"Sure." Finn yawned and handed the pages back to Troy. "Did you really come all the way over here just to share that?"

"I guess." The reality was that Troy had been sitting at home, thinking of Finn and scanning the pages of Brill's journal, when it occurred to him that he'd be a lot happier if he were working on the project while in the same room as Finn. The discovery of the name of the kid was, he knew, a pretty flimsy excuse to get on the subway. On the other hand, he'd had a lot of oddball thoughts that afternoon, and it seemed useful to toss a few at Finn to see what he'd think. He figured Finn would put down his crazier ideas. "I was doing some thinking this afternoon."

"No good can come from that."

"Ha." Troy playfully punched Finn's arm. "I was just wondering if the ghosts maybe chose me. Chose us."

"Chose you?"

"Sure. I mean, I'm gay, right? And I'm a scholar. Maybe they thought I'd be in a unique position to understand what they went through, in a way prior residents of the building weren't, plus I have the means to investigate. Maybe they're, I don't know, gaining strength as we do more digging into their lives, the way Maura said. I called her this afternoon and proposed my theory about me being chosen by the ghosts, and she seemed to think it was sound."

"Well, of course she did." Finn rolled his eyes.

Troy sat back up. "I don't know. I feel like we shouldn't count anything out. If they can manipulate you into mauling me on the chaise longue, maybe they manipulated me into starting to research the mystery to begin with."

Finn looked down at the bed for a moment, and then at Troy with an eyebrow raised. "Do you think they can manipulate our feelings?"

"I don't know. Sometimes I'm convinced they can; sometimes I'm sure they can't. Why?"

"Well, I really hated you before. Now I don't."

"I don't think you really hated me."

Finn huffed. "Well, we didn't get along, how's that?"

Troy wanted to correct him. Sure, they had some animosity, but Troy had always thought that the explosive sex spoke to some sort of mutual respect. But he could concede that they didn't always agree. "Okay."

"And now I have feelings for you. Really strong ones. Which doesn't make any sense, because, seriously, if I'd assembled a list of people I knew that I was likely to end up falling for, you'd be at the bottom."

"Gee, thanks."

"I'm a little worried, is all. What if none of this is real? What if my feelings for you are the ghosts' machinations?"

Although there was a tiny part of Troy that also was concerned this might be the case, deep down, he didn't really believe that. "Come on, Finn, that's crazy. And a month ago, you didn't even think the ghosts were real!"

"Well, now I know otherwise! Isn't that what researchers do? Evaluate evidence? The evidence I've seen seems to indicate that ghosts are real and are capable of manipulating thoughts and feelings."

"Maybe they temporarily manipulate your thinking, but they can't control how we feel about each other. Maura said it's more likely that they're exploiting feelings we already had."

"I'm not so sure about that. It suits their purpose to keep us working together. Despite everything, we make a good research team. They could be tricking us into thinking we like each other so that we keep working to solve the mystery."

"But Finn, I..."

"Prove me wrong, Troy."

Troy leaned over and kissed him. The kiss went immediately from a meeting of lips to an attempt to consume each other. Finn's teeth scraped along Troy's lower lip, and Troy's tongue probed Finn's mouth.

Troy said, "My feelings for you are real."

Finn pulled away and flopped back down on the bed. "How can I know that? How do I know that any of this is real?"

Troy backed away and considered. There was really only one solution. "I think we have to get rid of the ghosts."

"What?"

"You want proof that what we feel is real? We have to take the ghosts out of the equation. If we get rid of the ghosts, then what remains has to be real. Right?"

Finn looked surprised. "Okay. That's... surprisingly logical. So how do you propose we do it?"

Chapter 16

Cars roared over the Gowanus Expressway, creating a fuzz of noise that descended on them. Troy grabbed a reluctant Finn's hand and pulled him along 32nd Street in Brooklyn. "Maura said the shop was right... Oh, here we go."

It looked like any other junk shop from the outside, if you ignored the dark purple awning over the top, which read ESSENTIALS FOR MYSTICS.

"Of all your harebrained, crazy ideas, this is right up there," Finn said. He stopped walking but didn't let go of Troy's hand, which forced Troy to stop. "Bad enough that you talk me into researching ghosts and visiting a spiritualist, but now we're going into an occult shop to, what? Buy some potion that will make our ghosts go away?"

Troy opened his mouth and shut it again. He glanced through the storefront window, and then he looked down at his hand clasped with Finn's. "Maura says these guys are the best in Brooklyn."

"At what? Looking creepy?" The more Finn peered at the shop, the more he felt uncomfortable. The storefront window advertised potions and little dolls and all manner of weird things. There was a human skull in the corner of the display that Finn was pretty sure was not a fake.

"I'm supposed to talk to the owner to see if they have any products that will set the ghosts free. Apparently, supernatural elements are repelled by certain smells."

"This sounds like a lot of nonsense."

"Which is what you said when I told you there were ghosts to begin with, and look at where we are now."

Finn squeezed Troy's hand because he didn't know what else to do. Something in him really did not want to go into that store, despite his initial thinking that it would be kind of a fun interlude. When Troy came to him with the idea, he was so tickled with the thought of playing around with whatever wizardry existed in a shop like this that he had consented to tag along. Now that they were there, though, he found it hard to move his feet forward.

"I'm doing this for you, you know," said Troy.

Finn looked up at him. "I never asked you to look up occult shops on the Internet."

"You told me to prove I'm in love with you. That's what I'm doing. You will not be convinced until the ghosts are gone. Thus, I am getting rid of the ghosts."

"Love?" Finn frowned at that. Troy had said he had feelings; he'd never said he was in love.

"Yes, you idiot. I am in love with you. More than that, I'm convinced the ghosts have nothing to do with how I feel. And I know you feel the same way, so don't bother denying it."

Finn balked and pulled his hand away. "You don't know anything."

"I know plenty." Troy put his hands on his hips. "Come on, stop being stubborn and think about how you feel. I don't need the words right now, but I wish you wouldn't fight it so hard. You standing there denying it doesn't do either of us any good."

Finn hadn't denied it, had he? And was he in love with Troy?

It started to drizzle, and droplets got tangled up in Troy's dark hair. Troy didn't seem to notice. He stood there, looking a little menacing, in point of fact, the sleeves on his shirt straining against the muscles of his arms. He had on a white-and-blue striped button-down shirt undone at the collar, tucked into an expensive-looking and neatly pressed pair of khakis. He looked like a generic office worker out of central casting, except for the broad chest and the dark-rimmed glasses and the furrowed-brow angry expression on his face.

Finn loved every part of him.

He grunted. "Fine," he said.

Troy's expression softened. "I probably could have chosen a more romantic location for my deep confession than under the fucking highway in the rain."

"In front of an occult store."

"Yeah." Troy bit his lip. "I give up. Forget I said anything."

"No, Troy, I…"

"I don't need the words now, Finn. Let's just go inside. The rain is starting to stick to my glasses."

Finn followed Troy into the store. There was a large woman behind the counter wearing a willowy black dress. Her dark hair was pulled away from her face and kept in place with what looked like chopsticks with skulls on the ends. Piercings lined her ears and her eyebrow, nose, and lip. The store was otherwise empty. "Hello," she said.

"Hi," said Troy. "I'm a friend of Maura Higham's. She sent me down here to see if you had something that could help us, uh, get rid of some ghosts."

The woman perked up a little, and she and Troy started chatting about exorcisms, so Finn decided to wander around the store. There was a whole aisle of what looked like cleaning products. Finn picked up a bottle: *Después de Muerte brand Ghost Chaser*. Next to it was a green bottle: *Ghost-B-Gone with St. John's Wort!*

The woman walked toward Finn with Troy in tow. "Customers have had success with a combination of incense and herbs," she said as she walked by Finn. He followed, and they arrived at the end of an aisle. The woman sorted through a box full of packets of incense and handed a few to Troy. "Try these first. Burn one stick of each at the same time. It's the combination of scents that will drive the ghosts away."

She moved through the store to a display on the wall full of what Finn thought were voodoo dolls, most of them made of cloth with faces that looked like smiling skulls. She picked up a string of beads and said, "Hang these over the main door to your house. It creates a gateway through which the ghosts will leave." She moved away again, toward a display of books near the register. She picked one up and handed it to Finn. "And if those don't work, this is what many consider to be the authoritative text on how to exorcise ghosts."

Finn turned the book—*Showing the Light: How to Help the Lost Get to the Next Plane*—over in his hands and was about to put it back when he noticed that Troy had put the beads and incense on the counter and was reaching for his wallet.

"Seriously?" Finn asked. He put the book next to Troy's purchases. "You're buying me lunch too."

* * *

They had lunch at a Chinese restaurant in Sunset Park. Finn spent the first half of the meal flipping through *Showing the Light*, occasionally reading aloud passages he thought were especially ridiculous but otherwise seeming to take a keen interest in the material. Troy figured Finn really had a keen interest in not talking about their feelings. This was probably just as well. He felt like an idiot for telling Finn he loved him earlier, frustrated that he'd been provoked into it instead of saying the words at a more appropriate moment.

He picked at his chicken and vegetable dish, and then, for lack of anything else to do, he pulled some scans of Brill's journal out of his bag. He'd brought them to read on the subway that morning but had been too preoccupied with Finn. Now that Finn was pretending to ignore him, he supposed he might as well focus his attention on something useful.

They each read silently for a while until Troy came across a name he hadn't seen before. "Hey, Finn."

"So this guy thinks ghosts are the remaining souls of people who died with unfinished business."

Troy was surprised by Finn saying something so off-topic from what he was about to say. "Uh, okay. Unfinished business like what?"

"The author's suggestions are things like a love interest who never knew they were loved or monetary affairs left unsettled."

"Or, possibly, an unsolved murder."

"I suppose that would be a logical conclusion, yes."

"I just read something interesting. You want to know what I found?"

Finn put the book down. "Okay, what?"

"New player. In 1876, Brill met a man named Beauchamp, and he doesn't like him much at all. Beauchamp is some kind of activist, I think. He seems to want money from Brill to support some sort of cause, but Brill's journal is vague on the particulars."

"Worth looking into," Finn said, though there wasn't much oomph in his voice. He looked at the plate of food in front of him like he hadn't noticed it there previously.

"Yeah, I'm making a note to see if he's mentioned again after this excerpt."

"I think Cutler mentioned a Beauchamp in a section I read recently. Might be a coincidence. Let me see if they're spelled the same." He gestured for Troy to hand him the pages.

Troy relinquished his photocopies. "I think if the last few weeks have taught us anything, it's that nothing is coincidence."

"Oh, come on. This wouldn't be the first false lead we've chased."

"No, but it's the first lead that has shown up in both journals, assuming you're right. And have you noticed that we tend to come across significant things at the same time?"

"Because we're reading the journals in chronological order."

"Yes, but this could mean something! Our both finding the same thing, I mean."

Finn put the pages back on the table. His face became flush. "Seriously, what are the odds?"

"Jesus, Finn. Need I remind you about that whole kiss thing? That wasn't a coincidence."

"Right. There are no coincidences. Except you and I met by chance when were in college because you were working in the library and I had an assignment that involved looking at materials in the Rare Book collection. Are you going to tell me now that fate is responsible for my professor assigning me that project and then me choosing to go to the library while you were working? That the ghosts inspired you to be extra antagonistic with me?"

"No, of course not."

But Finn was on a roll now. "Next, you'll probably tell me that my enrolling at Columbia was orchestrated by a couple of ghosts so that maybe, someday, we'd end up in the same building at the same time and team up to solve their murder!"

Finn's raised voice drew the attention from the other diners in the otherwise quiet restaurant. Troy was annoyed; just when they were making progress, Finn had to go and be all difficult again. Troy shushed him. Then he stage-whispered, "I never suggested that. You're being ridiculous. All I meant was that you should entertain the possibility that this name has some significance. I realize that there are probably several dozen people named Beauchamp in New York City in 1876, but, given how things have gone with this project so far, I think it's worth spending five minutes considering the possibility that this one is important."

Finn grunted. "Fine," he said.

"You know, I never believed in any of this fate stuff either. I think it probably is chance that we met at all to begin with, but it makes sense that our paths have crossed over the years since we both work within a small network of Gilded Age historians in New York City. As for the rest, well, I don't know. Keep an open mind? Look, maybe it's nothing. Maybe Beauchamp doesn't mean anything. But maybe he does."

"I feel sometimes like we're bit players in a larger drama," said Finn.

"What does that mean?"

Finn picked up his chopsticks and stabbed a piece of broccoli. "Everything is shit. Bad enough that I wound up in the same PhD program as Troy the Wonder Boy who left a trail of success and sparkles everywhere he went, but then I lost my funding and couldn't even finish. Then I have to drop out of my masters program because my boyfriend cheated on me and I didn't have the guts to go back. I wind up as a research assistant for a crazy lady who's got me working sixty-hour weeks, a job that puts me back in contact with goddamn Troy the Wonder Boy, and somehow I decide to help him solve a mystery that doesn't make one fucking bit of sense."

"No need to talk about me in the third person. I'm sitting right here."

Finn leveled his gaze at Troy. "And now I've got this goddamn ghost in my head who is trying to help us solve the mystery, only I'm more confused than ever, because somehow he's got me convinced that I'm in love with you, but that doesn't make any sense because I'm supposed to hate you." He sighed. "I did hate you, for a long time. I blamed a lot of my failures on you. That was easy. This—" He gestured to the space between them. "This is hard."

Bingo. "Yeah."

Finn rubbed his eyes. "And now you expect me to believe this bullshit that one mention of some dude's name is going to crack open the murder investigation?"

"That's not what I said. I just thought it was worth looking into. I don't know what you're getting all worked up about." Although Troy had a good idea. It was the same thing that had been occupying his thoughts for the better part of the last few days.

Finn's eyebrows knit together. "Fine, we'll look into it."

"Do you have access to anything through Loretta that might prove relevant? Name databases, anything like that?"

Finn shrugged. "Maybe."

"Indulge me and see what you can find out."

"Loretta has me researching the players in the Woodhull drama who were buried in Green-Wood Cemetery. I've been talking to the historian there. My ancestors are buried there, actually. The Finnegans. And there are a lot of them. We're Irish Catholic, after all."

"Really? Brill and Cutler were buried there too, I believe. Maybe we should pay a visit to Green-Wood."

Finn sighed. "Well, if nothing else, this project is taking me to all corners of Brooklyn."

"That's the spirit!" Troy felt a little daring and like perhaps Finn's façade was cracking a little. He reached across the table and took Finn's hand. Finn responded by squeezing his fingers before he glanced around the restaurant, and by some mutual understanding that they didn't want any harassment, they parted. Troy felt like maybe they'd come to an agreement, though.

Chapter 17

It felt a little like decorating for Christmas. Finn acted as spotter for Troy as he stood on a stepladder and strung beads over the main entrance to the Brill House. The beads were green and yellow and sparkled a little in the sunlight streaming in from the windows off the lobby.

It was a Tuesday, so the Brill House was closed to the public, which was just as well because Finn thought this whole endeavor was a little ridiculous. Could Troy have really thought beads and some incense would scare off the ghosts? He sure seemed to, and he worked with intense determination.

Troy took a nail from his pocket and lined it up with the door frame. He held up a hammer and said, "How did you manage to escape Loretta's clutches, anyway?"

"If anyone asks, I'm at the Brooklyn Public Library right now."

"Clever."

"I did actually call Darnell this morning and asked him to put together some things for me. Although, it turns out that the one biography of Woodhull that Loretta most wants is checked out and overdue."

"That bites." Troy gave the nail a couple of good taps before checking that it was secure.

"Checked out by you."

Troy looked down. "Oh, right. I forgot I checked that out."

Troy's casual tone pissed Finn off—was Troy really so disorganized that he forgot?—but he tried to make his voice sound neutral. "When did you check it out?"

Troy looped the beads over the nail he'd just placed. "Uh. Right after you came here for your tour, I guess. I was curious about Woodhull."

"It's out of print. This is the only copy of the book in any library or bookstore in the city. It includes some controversial information about Woodhull that may or may not have evidence to back it up, and Loretta loves a controversy. She demanded I get the book. So of course you have it."

"Help me down."

Troy motioned for Finn to step closer and then borrowed his shoulder to lean against as he climbed back down the ladder. Finn instinctively reached out a hand and placed it on Troy's back. When Troy's feet were firmly on the floor, he realized he was touching Troy tenderly and then remembered he was mad about the book. He stepped away.

"I mean, of fucking course, you have the book."

"I'm not sabotaging you," Troy said. "The book is in my apartment somewhere. You're welcome to it as soon as we finish here. I'll call Darnell and see if he can check it out to you." He put the hammer on the information desk. "Look, you want to know the truth? I went to the library right after you came here for the tour, and I found the only biography of Woodhull in the stacks. I read it because you were researching Woodhull."

"So now you're suddenly interested in Woodhull?"

"I'm interested in *you*, dumb-ass."

Finn knew he should have found that less surprising than he did, because Troy had already made his feelings quite clear. Still, he took another step back and said, "Oh."

"Yeah, *oh*." Troy walked over to the information desk, where he'd left the bag of supplies from the occult store. "Why do I bother? You stubbornly cling to this notion that I'm your enemy, but I'm really not. Quite the opposite, in fact. I thought we were past this now. Why do you still do that?"

Finn plopped himself in the chair behind the desk. He supposed he could make something up or dodge the question. He also supposed he could just tell the truth. "I don't know. Because it's easier to be mad at you than to be in love with you?"

Troy's eyes widened for a moment, but he recovered quickly. "Why do you think that is?"

Finn couldn't look at Troy, so he looked at the display of pamphlets on the information desk. He took a moment to gather his thoughts. He wasn't usually prone to making grand speeches, but that was what this situation seemed to call for. "Because love is a risk, I guess. Because I've already put so much energy into trying to impress you, and all of my efforts failed spectacularly. I mean, it's always been you, I guess, the one person in the world that I really wanted to show I was smart and successful, but I'm neither of those things, as it turns out. And the one time I put myself out there for a guy, I got my heart stomped on. I can't stand the thought of…" Finn swallowed to keep his emotion from showing. "It's probably the ghosts talking, but it turns out I actually like spending time around you, even when we're arguing. I don't want to risk you."

Finn couldn't see Troy but felt him nearby. There was a long silence before Troy took a step closer. "Would you listen to yourself? Have you always felt this way?"

Finn looked at him out of the corner of his eye. "I

guess you got under my skin when I first met you. And something in me always wanted to best the Wonder Boy. Not for romantic reasons, but just because you pissed me off. I wanted to be better, smarter. Then, somewhere in there, it became about impressing you specifically, wanting you to know I was on your level or better. But everything I tried, I failed at. My GPA was always a little lower than yours. Most of my professors couldn't remember my name. I had to drop out of the same PhD program that you completed in record time. Then I had to drop out of library school, so after almost four years of graduate work, I still only have a BA and a job as a research assistant to a woman who drives me bananas. I'm thirty-two years old, and I'm nothing."

Troy walked around the desk and stood next to Finn's chair. "No, you're everything." He knelt next to the chair and touched Finn's knee. "I told you, I already thought you were smart, but if I didn't, you certainly proved yourself working with me on this mystery. You don't need to impress me. I'm already impressed. I mean, you're stubborn as hell, and you have a short fuse, but you're also clever and funny and attractive, and you can be caring and thoughtful when you want to be. I don't care about your academic credentials. I care about *you*, and the stuff that impresses me about you is not the sort of stuff you can get a piece of paper certifying." Troy leaned up and kissed Finn's cheek. "You get under my skin a lot too. It's why I think you're worth the effort and the risk."

"I don't understand any of this," Finn said, finally looking at Troy. "I was so mad when it turned out you were the curator here, and I didn't even want to get involved in this project at all, but now we're making these big emotional speeches? How did that happen?"

"We grew up and got over ourselves? Maybe you were

finally honest about what you felt?"

"I want to be with you, Troy." Finn felt that down in his gut. He was already mourning the inevitable day when they wouldn't be working together anymore. Monday nights with Troy had come to be the highlight of his week, and now that he was spending almost all of his free time on this project, it was going to feel like a large void when it ended. "But how do I know that what I feel is real and not the machinations of a couple of ghosts who are using us to get some kind of closure?"

Troy stood up. "Hopefully we're about to find that out."

He told Finn to stay put then disappeared into his office. He returned a minute later with a ceramic contraption and a matchbook. "I had a Buddhist roommate a few years ago who used to burn incense all the time. He left this behind. I think it'll do the job." He put it on the information desk and pulled the packages of incense from the bag.

"Kinda looks like a bong," Finn said.

"Yes, well. It'll hold a couple of incense sticks, won't it?" Troy pulled one incense stick from each of the packets and arranged them in the ceramic thing.

Finn stood up and walked over to Troy. He put a hand on Troy's arm. "Hey, just in case this turns out to be the end…"

"The end of what?" Troy asked. He stopped what he was doing and turned toward Finn.

"This project. Us. All of it. I just wanted to say, I've enjoyed our time together."

"Is this a breakup?"

"No, I just… I mean, if the ghosts leave, and we go

back to feeling whatever we were feeling before this whole thing started, if we go back to finding each other annoying, if we stop feeling what we do now, if that happens, I just want you to know—"

"Finn, I..." Instead of completing his thought, Troy pulled Finn into a tight hug. Finn put his arms around Troy and sighed into his shoulder. It felt so good just to be held in those strong arms.

"Let's give this a shot," said Troy.

He flashed the matchbook at Finn; it advertised a gay bar they'd frequented when they were in grad school that had long since closed. Finn opened his mouth to comment, but Troy pulled a match out of the book, struck it, and lit the first stick of incense.

"It's this combination of scents that should drive off our ghosts," said Troy.

Troy lit the second stick of incense. He moved toward the third but then hesitated. He pulled the match from the book and stared at it. Then he turned to Finn and planted a kiss on his lips. Finn met him happily but wondered in the back of his mind if he'd ever feel this way again, if he'd still want to kiss Troy after the ghosts were gone, if this was the last kiss they'd ever share. He opened his mouth and deepened the kiss, dragged it out, wanted it to last.

The earth seemed to move, but then Finn realized the floor was *actually* shaking. It shook hard enough that he was jostled free of Troy's grasp. His pulse kicked up, and he looked around in alarm.

"Something's definitely happening," Finn said. The ghosts had his attention, for sure. The shaking floor jostled him, and he was afraid things were about to get a lot worse.

Troy didn't seem as scared. "No joke." He struck

another match and then lit the last stick of incense.

There was a blast of light so intense it felt like an explosion. Finn and Troy both fell backward, landing side by side on the floor of the lobby. Finn's back throbbed from the impact. He cried out, both in pain and in fear. Bits of plaster rained down from the ceiling. *Shit, the whole building is going to come down!*

The front door blew open. The ghosts seemed to be gaining power, if they were able to push the door open with that much force. Finn watched the door closely, wondering if the ghosts were on their way out, but then the beads fell from the door and the incense was instantly reduced to dust. Finn's heart pounded, but he was too afraid to move.

"Jesus Christ," said Troy, scrambling to his feet.

A wind blew through the lobby, sending pens and paper flying. A high-pitched shriek tore through the air at an ear-piercing volume. Something fell on Finn's head and covered his eyes. It had to be the sweater from the back of Genevieve's chair. He tugged on it, but it wouldn't move, and he panicked because he couldn't see. Troy gasped and cried out. Then there was a thud.

Something hard pelted Finn's arm. It stung where it hit. The lights flickered through the sweater. He yanked on a sleeve. He needed to see that Troy was okay. The sweater clung to his face.

The front door slammed shut, the lights went out, and the air stopped moving. Finn pulled the sweater off and looked around. Everything that had been swirling around was now on the floor. He saw Troy, lying on his back looking stunned. Blood trickled from a cut on his forehead; Finn couldn't see any other injuries but still worried Troy might be seriously hurt. Finn crawled over to him.

"Are you okay?" Finn tried to get a closer look at the cut.

"Yeah, I think so. A book came out of nowhere and hit me in the head. It surprised me so much that I fell."

"Can you move?"

"Yeah." Troy struggled a little but managed to sit up. "Holy shit. That was not what I expected to happen." He surveyed the room. "I guess we need to pick all this up now."

Finn grabbed a tissue from the box that had conveniently landed on the floor next to him and blotted Troy's cut. "You think the ghosts are gone?"

"Hard to say. Do you feel any different?"

Finn paused to examine himself and found that, no, he felt the same. He looked at Troy, who smiled weakly. Well, that was something. Looking at Troy still made his pulse race. Or maybe that was the subsiding panic. Either way, that seemed to indicate his feelings were still there.

He leaned down and kissed the cut on Troy's forehead. Troy murmured, "I take that to mean you don't hate me."

"I don't hate you."

"I don't hate you either." He reached over and pulled Finn into his arms. "Good to know my efforts did not go to waste."

Something like rain fell on Finn's head. He looked up. Gray dust was falling on them. "What the hell?"

"I think it's the incense." With some effort, Troy stood up and offered Finn a hand.

"That cut looks bad."

"The corner of the book cover caught me. I think it's okay." Troy touched it, and his fingers came away with a drop of blood. "Well, nothing a bandage won't cure." He looked around. "I didn't burn that much incense. Why is there so much in the room?"

The dust in the air started to swirl. Finn's heartbeat sped up again.

"The ghosts are still here," Troy said.

"Looks that way."

"So we haven't repelled them so much as severely pissed them off."

As if in answer, all of the books behind the information desk poured off the shelves. The dust from the incense formed a tornado cloud in the middle of the room and the papers started to spin again.

Finn tried to jump out of the way, but the swirling debris followed him. Finn's heart was pumping with fear and adrenaline, but he had no idea how to stop what they'd started.

Troy grabbed Finn's hand. He shouted, "I'm sorry! I wanted you to have peace! To go on to the next plane! I didn't mean to make you angry. I want to help! What can I do?"

Out of nowhere, a sheet of newspaper flew through the air and slapped Troy in the face. Finn grabbed it before it fell to the floor. The headline read, TWO BROOKLYN MEN FOUND DEAD AT RESIDENCE. The paper was dated July 17, 1878.

"Remember that bit in the book we bought that said ghosts were souls with unfinished business?"

Troy looked around the room, alarm on his face. "I remember."

Finn handed Troy the newspaper article. "Maybe in

order to let them go, we have to finish their business. We have to solve the mystery. If we find their killer, they will be able to leave."

As soon as the words were out of Finn's mouth, all activity in the room stopped. The dust vanished, the lights came back on, and everything swirling through the air fell to the floor.

"I'll take that as a yes," said Troy. He took a deep breath and turned to Finn. "I think we have our answer."

"Yeah." Finn breathed slowly to get the pace of his heart back down to normal. "Back to work."

"Come on, help me clean this up."

Finn let go of Troy's hand and walked to the bookcase. He started putting the books back. "I still have to go to the library," he said. "They close at five today, so get a move on."

"Right." Troy picked up stray papers. "Come home with me afterward, and I'll give you the Woodhull book. I'll even pay the overdue fine."

"Charitable of you."

"If it sweetens the deal at all, we could order delivery. I think I've got beer and ice cream too. And there's always the raunchy sex on the floor of my living room."

Finn laughed. "Okay, okay. After we finish up here, we'll go pay Darnell a visit. Then I have to call Loretta. But after that, I think I can work some dinner and raunchy sex into my schedule."

"Good." Troy walked to Finn and dropped a kiss on his nose. Then he started picking up paper again. He picked up a pile of brochures and placed them back in their plastic holder. "You know," he said to the ceiling, "the least you could do is help us clean up."

The ghosts were silent.

* * *

Finn led the way into the Brooklyn Room at the library. Troy leaned on the desk and started humming the "1812 Overture," which caught Darnell's attention. He smiled at his guests.

"Hello, gentlemen. I will be right with you." He walked to the back of the room and rummaged through a stack of media.

Troy grinned at Finn, who was across the room looking at a display of old maps. Finn looked up, and their eyes met. He smiled. *Yup*, Troy thought. *I'm still completely smitten.* It was a nice feeling.

"Okay," said Darnell, dropping a pile of books and papers on his desk. "Finnie, I've got those books you requested and photocopies of the documents you wanted."

Finn walked back to the counter. "Thanks, D, I appreciate it."

"Not a problem. Things have been a little slow around here lately. You gave me something to do today. And speaking of things to do, I got an e-mail saying a Green-Wood Cemetery historian is giving a talk at the KCHS tomorrow. Will you be there, Helen?"

"Yeah," said Troy. "I have to give a presentation to drum up interest in the Brill House. The KCHS figures anyone dorky enough to come hear about a cemetery is probably also interested in a big ol' haunted house."

"Good. I will put in an appearance and pretend to be interested in the Brill House." Darnell grinned. "What happened to your forehead?"

Troy touched the cut. The only bandages they'd been

able to find had cartoon characters on them, and Troy had thought leaving the cut naked was less conspicuous. He'd let Finn clean it instead, and though it stung when Finn put some first-aid cream on it, he was happy enough to let Finn stroke his face. They'd made out a little in the bathroom at the Brill House. Just a taste of what was to come later, he thought.

"Helen had a run-in with a book." Finn chuckled. "It's a shame that his ship-launching face is so marred, isn't it?"

"The pen proves mightier than the sword then after all, eh?" said Darnell. His gaze traveled between Finn and Troy. "You boys look awfully cozy together."

Troy threw an arm around Finn and said, "Temporary ceasefire."

Darnell raised an eyebrow. "Right." He shuffled through the pile of stuff on the desk. "My invitation to your wedding better be embossed, is all I'm saying. Finn, the books have to get checked out the old-fashioned way, either at the machine or the circulation desk downstairs, but the photocopies are yours. We're supposed to charge five cents a copy, but I'll waive the fee, seeing as how we're old friends and all."

Finn wriggled away from Troy and picked up the pile of books. "Thank you. I appreciate it."

"Tell Loretta I want a mention on her acknowledgements page."

Chapter 18

Loretta had Finn putting together an extensive set of genealogy charts for Woodhull. He hit a wall when he got to the generation before her grandparents and so was in the process of tracking down her descendants when it occurred to him he might be able to use the same database to find some information on the players in the Brill House mystery. He ran a few names but didn't come up with much. He was feeling tired and frustrated, not making much progress, preoccupied with Troy and wondering what the hell to do about their ghost problem, when Loretta flounced into the room.

"Did your dog just die?" she asked.

Finn plastered a smile on his face. "No, everything's fine. Just hitting a wall. Woodhull's family wasn't so great at record keeping."

Loretta scrunched up her nose, an expression Finn thought of as her displeased face. "Well. I'm going to need some caffeine if I'm going to finish this chapter. Could you run down to that café on the corner?"

Finn accepted her money and went outside. As he walked to the café, he dialed Troy from his cell phone.

Troy answered, "Hello, darling."

The endearment threw him off, but he said, "Hi." He related what he'd just learned by running searches, which was not much. He walked into the café as he finished his explanation and ordered Loretta's usual midafternoon pick-me-up—a high-calorie latte contraption—and a plain old normal coffee for himself.

It occurred to him that there wasn't a real need to call

Troy, since Finn had found so little relevant information, but he'd wanted to anyway, just to hear his voice. Leaving the office seemed like as good an excuse as any.

"Thanks for trying." Troy was silent for a moment. Right about the time Finn was handed his coffee, he added, "This is disappointing. I feel like we're running into a lot dead of ends now. I have a few more ideas, though."

Finn went back outside with two coffee cups tucked into a cardboard carrier. "Okay. I gotta go back to work, but I thought I'd let you know."

"Yeah, thanks. Are you doing anything tonight that's not work? We could get dinner or something. My treat."

"Did you just ask me out on a date?"

"Finn, darling. Let me explain something to you."

"If this is a birds-and-the-bees talk, save your breath."

"Sometimes, when a boy likes another boy *in that way*, he takes him out and they eat together on the pretense of getting to know each other before they have sex. That is what I would like to do with you."

"Okay. Thank you for clarifying."

"So? Is it a date?"

Finn stood at the entrance to Loretta's building. "Yeah, fine. It's a date. Are we dating?"

"We're fucking on a regular basis. That's kind of the same."

Finn laughed. "Sure."

They made plans to meet at a restaurant near Finn's apartment before Finn bowed out of the conversation. He realized as he rode the elevator up to Loretta's apartment that he couldn't stop smiling.

* * *

Troy beat Finn to the restaurant. The place had been Finn's recommendation, and it was a surprisingly romantic one. It was a little French bistro with lush decor—rich red walls, crisp white tablecloths, silver candelabras on each table—and Troy wondered if Finn maybe had a little romance in mind.

He got a table and ordered a glass of wine while he waited. He was feeling glad that he hadn't gone home to change into more casual clothes; he'd had meetings all day and still had on his suit.

Finn was ten minutes late. And, bless him, he had on a blue oxford shirt untucked over a nice pair of charcoal gray pants. This was dressed up for Finn. Now Troy was more convinced than ever that there was romance on the agenda, and a pleasant warmth settled in his chest.

Finn slid into a chair. He shot Troy a tired smile.

"I'm surprised you didn't bring me flowers," Troy said.

Finn furrowed his brow.

"I mean, the candles, the mood lighting, the fact that you're wearing nice pants instead of jeans. If I didn't know better, I'd wonder if you weren't trying to get in my pants."

"I *am* trying to get in your pants."

"This is all very romantic. Although, if you propose, I'm gonna have to say no."

Finn looked around, and his eyes widened. "Oh. Right. This is what I get for picking a restaurant when I'm tired. This place just opened, like, a month ago. Janice and I ate here right after it opened and really liked the food. I don't think I noticed how schmaltzy the decor was because it was Janice, you know? Not a date."

That disappointed Troy. And here he'd thought Finn was trying. He smiled, not wanting Finn to see that he was hurt. "You wound me, Finn. Here I thought you were trying to wine and dine me to show your affection."

Finn laughed. "Well, maybe I wanted to impress you a little. I mean, the food here *is* good. But I live down the block from a pizza place. Would you have preferred that?"

"No."

The waiter came by, and Finn ordered a glass of wine.

Troy said, "Since you're a classless boor, maybe I'll be the romantic one tonight. I did ask you out on the date, after all." He raised his glass. "Let's toast."

"To?"

"To rekindled friendship. Or kindled friendship, I guess. To mysteries and their solutions. To us."

"All right. To us."

They clinked glasses. Troy took a sip of his wine and let it sit on his tongue, liking the sour fruity taste of it, before he swallowed. He watched Finn, examining his face while he perused the menu. Troy really liked the lines of Finn's face—the slant of his cheekbones, the point of his nose. He liked Finn's ruddy cheeks and the bit of scruffy stubble on his chin. He liked Finn's body, its rangy quality, the way clothes draped, the way it just *was* without being too self-conscious.

Finn looked at Troy over the top of the menu. "Are you checking me out?"

"You know I am."

Finn smiled and went back to perusing.

"I mean, I want to do this right," said Troy.

Finn put the menu down and looked at Troy. "Okay.

You seem to be doing pretty well so far. For what it's worth, you will get laid tonight."

Troy appreciated that. He also liked that he felt like he could say anything to Finn, that he could be honest. There was no game playing. "It's not just that. Getting laid is not that hard."

"Says you."

"Here's the thing. Attractive gay men in New York? Dime a dozen. I want to have sex with one particular man, and possibly only that man, for the foreseeable future. This is kind of a new thing for me, so I'll thank you not to make light of it."

Finn looked suitably chastened. He took a sip of his wine. "Okay."

"Because, the thing is, I love you. Enough so that it makes me want to be a one-man kind of guy. Enough to take you to fancy romantic dinners and real dates, you know? We've spent almost all of our time together poring over dusty books or fucking, so I thought I'd try something different. And I thought you felt the same until just now when you said you forgot this restaurant was kind of romantic."

The words came out sounding more wounded than Troy had intended. He picked up the menu and looked at it again to mask his emotion.

Finn didn't say anything for a while. Then he let out a breath. "My first instinct is to put you off because I've never been that good at relationships, but I don't want to lose you, and I know how circular that is, but—"

"Remember that whole conversation we had last week about risk?"

"I remember. I'm not sure if I'll be ready for the whole

committed flowers-and-chocolates thing until after the ghost mystery is resolved, but I guess I'm willing to give it a shot."

"I'm glad." Troy smiled.

"I feel like we did some of this backward. Don't people usually go on dates before they start having meaningful conversations like this?"

"Probably."

Finn shook his head. "I'm going to have to tell my friends I'm dating you. No one will believe it."

"Eh, I don't know about that."

A waiter came by and took their order. Finn sipped wine and stared into space, and Troy imagined he could see the moment when Finn started to relax finally, to unwind from the work day.

"How do you feel?" Troy asked.

Finn seemed confused by the question. He cocked his head. "I'm all right. Tired."

"How's Loretta?"

"She's…herself, I don't know. The book is coming along. Although now Loretta wants me to try to incorporate some of the information from my aborted dissertation. She's trying to make the argument that Woodhull was more essential to the suffrage movement than Elizabeth Cady Stanton, which seems like a stretch to me."

"Woodhull gave that speech to Congress, though, right? That was a pretty important moment for the movement."

"Did you just know that or did you actually read the Woodhull biography you tried to hide from me?"

Troy laughed. "Both. As a scholar of the latter half of the nineteenth century, I was aware of Woodhull's speeches and presidential run, but I did actually read that biography also. Fascinating stuff."

"I think what I'm learning is that she was way ahead of her time. Some of her beliefs seem downright mundane now but scandalized the crap out of people in her day."

"Kinda like the sweet little romance between two men that we've been researching?"

Finn smiled. "Yeah, kinda like that." He sipped his wine again. "Have you done anything recently that's not research?"

"Darnell took me to this sports bar in Chelsea a few days ago. I like the vibe there, and the bartenders seem to be required to be incredibly hot."

"Was this that new gay sports bar?"

"Indeed it was. You'll be happy to know that, while I did get hit on a lot, I tended to lose my would-be paramours when it became obvious that I know basically nothing about sports."

Finn opened his mouth. Then he closed it again and laughed. He shook his head. "I like to put on football games on Sundays when I'm working, mostly for background noise, but sometimes I'll get sucked into the game. I may not be very athletic, but I know a few things about sports. I was about to offer to teach you the basics, but then I realized you'd use this knowledge for evil. And by evil, I mean that you'd use it to pick up men."

Troy considered. "Well, maybe. I mean, it's true that if some swarthy gentleman came up to me at a sports bar all goals and home runs and blah blah, I'd probably try to impress him with my astounding knowledge of football."

"You could probably be convincing. You're built like a

linebacker. And football has touchdowns."

"Whatever. What if I don't want the swarthy gentleman in the sports bar?"

"That would be okay with me also."

Troy found Finn's face unreadable. If he was jealous, it didn't show.

Their food arrived, and conversation drifted around, from pop culture to their mutual friends. Troy loved that they never seemed to run out of things to talk about, which went a long way toward proving to him that the affection between them was real and not just the machinations of the ghosts. Maybe the ghosts had pushed them together, but those feelings had probably been there for a long time.

They finished dinner and left the restaurant. Finn started walking in the direction of his apartment, which Troy took as an invitation. He grabbed Finn's hand as they walked, and Finn intertwined his fingers with Troy's.

"This is nice," Troy said.

"Yeah."

And it was. Troy felt pretty safe holding hands in Finn's corner of the Lower East Side. It was nice, too, to be spending an evening with Finn where they weren't fighting or researching.

"Is your roommate home?"

"Nope," said Finn. "She told me this morning that she intends to spend tonight at her boyfriend's, so I should not wait up."

"Oh, interesting. So we could potentially do it on your couch."

"Uh, sure, if you really want to. Or we could go to my room, where there is a bed and less potential of getting, like, tweed burn."

Troy laughed. "Or that."

* * *

Troy had asked if he could have a few minutes to freshen up, so Finn had done a few chores, and he realized as he walked down the hall that he'd given Troy more time than he probably needed. He walked into his room and found Troy lounging naked on the bed, flipping through Finn's copy of the *American Historical Review*. Just the sight of the man had heat and arousal flowing through Finn's body.

"There's a review in here of your boss's last book. Fascinating stuff. I mean the review is fascinating. The author clearly thinks Loretta is a hack and comes up with a more creative way of saying so without saying it explicitly in each paragraph."

"Troy."

Troy closed the journal and put it on the bedside table. He stretched his arms over his head. "Well, since you decided cleaning your whole apartment was more important than having sex with me, I took the liberty of going through your bathroom. You sure own a lot of hair products."

"You told me you needed a few minutes. I just did the dishes I left out this morning."

"Right. Well." Troy patted the space on the bed next to him. "I monopolized your bathroom to take care of some other things too. I am clean inside and out, if you know what I mean." He waggled his eyebrows.

Finn almost fell over as desire crawled through his chest. He looked over Troy in all his naked splendor: the muscular body with the dusting of dark hair across his chest, the narrow waist, the defined abs, the very hard cock resting on his thigh. Finn's attraction to Troy made him dizzy, because there was not only this big strong body but also a handsome face with angular cheeks and those sexy dark-rimmed glasses perched on his nose, and Finn loved the whole package. Fortunately, Troy was there on his bed waiting for him. And, yes, Finn did know exactly what he meant.

"You just gonna stand there gawking or what?"

"You are so hot," Finn squeaked out.

Troy laughed. "So, we're going with gawking." He pulled his glasses off and placed them on the bedside table. Then he grabbed his own cock and started stroking. "And here I am, dressed to party but no one to party with."

"You're killing me." Finn pulled his own shirt off over his head.

Troy whistled. "You can do better than that. Put a little shimmy into it."

"I'm not doing a strip tease for you."

"Party pooper."

Finn would have indulged Troy's every wish, but the simple act of taking his clothes off in a seductive way embarrassed him a little. But then Troy was really getting into jerking off, and Finn knew he couldn't let him get away with that. He undid the top button on his pants and inched the zipper down. Troy stared. So Finn gave him a little show. He managed to tamp down his embarrassment and took his sweet time pulling his pants down, revealing himself bit by bit. He grabbed his own hard cock through his underwear and gave it a squeeze for Troy's benefit. He felt ridiculous, but Troy seemed riveted, watching and stroking and hooting when Finn did something he especially liked.

As a last act, Finn slowly pushed his briefs down his

legs, watching Troy jerk off the whole time, and the vision before him was so hot that lust overcame his embarrassment.

"You are one sexy man, Christopher Finnegan," Troy said. "Come here."

Finn crawled onto the bed and was immediately pulled into Troy's arms. His cock slid against Troy's, making him shiver with delight. He kissed Troy and got an eager response, and soon they were both grabbing and groping and groaning.

Finn pulled away. "Let me fuck you."

Troy held up a condom and a bottle of lube. "I went through your drawers too. You have boring taste in porn."

"How long did I leave you here?" Finn grabbed the condom and put it on. His whole body seemed to be honing in on one purpose: fucking Troy until he could no longer speak.

Because now Troy was getting annoying. Troy said, "The overproduced movies with those big muscle guys, they're so generic."

Finn upended the bottle of lube and got a fair amount all over his fingers. Without much prelude, he shoved Troy's legs open and pushed two fingers into his body.

Troy grunted but said, "Again."

"Shut up about the porn," said Finn. "You sure as hell better not have a problem with me liking big muscle guys."

Troy hooked his hands under his knees and pulled them to his chest, giving Finn better access. Finn added a third finger, then curled them to hit Troy's prostate. Finn was rewarded when Troy let out a high-pitched moan, and his eyes rolled to the back of his head. "God, right *there*."

Troy's breathing became erratic, and his whole body

seemed to push against Finn's hand. Finn could tell he was getting close, but he wasn't ready for Troy to come quite yet. He withdrew his hand, the act of which pulled a displeased mewl from Troy. He was about to change tactics when Troy rolled over on top of him. He was temporarily knocked out of breath by the force of Troy's weight suddenly pressing against him. He liked it, though, liked the weight and pressure and how solid Troy was. He smelled Troy, sweat, cologne, soap, and man, and he reached up.

They kissed. Their tongues waged battle, pushing into each other's mouths, pushing against each other. Their skin pressed together. Finn loved the feel of Troy pressing him into the mattress, of all that strength looming above him. He licked a line down Troy's chin, his tongue rubbing against the stubble there, tasting salty sweat and whatever magic there was in Troy that had Finn half out of his mind with arousal.

Then Troy pulled away a little bit, sitting up and straddling Finn's hips. He reached behind him and grabbed Finn's cock, then held it as he moved his body back. The anticipation of what was about to happen made Finn's blood rush. Troy sat, pulling Finn's cock into his body. That body was warm and tight and amazing. Troy went still for a moment, but his face gave him away. Troy was utterly beautiful, wrapped up in his own ecstasy, his mouth open, a desperate look in his eyes. Finn wanted more, wanted to move, wanted to draw this out and make it last. He gently bucked his hips.

"Yes," Troy whispered.

Finn pivoted his hips up, sliding farther into Troy. His pulse jumped as Troy's hot body squeezed him. But Troy took control, setting the pace, lifting up, then sitting back down, a hand pressed to Finn's chest as he moved. Troy's fingers traveled to Finn's nipples and pinched. Pain jolted through Finn's body as Troy's nails dug into his skin, but the pain was exciting, arousing, and sent jolts through his body straight to his cock.

Finn's skin tingled, his back arched, and everything about this was completely overwhelming: the way Troy moved, the way he slid inside, the smell, the sound of skin slapping together. Finn grabbed Troy's cock and stroked, loving the feeling of that hot flesh in his hand. Troy whimpered. He put one hand on Finn's chest to steady himself and pulled at his hair with the other. Finn breathed erratically, beads of sweat trickling over his body. He wanted to come, wanted release, knew it was close, and he wanted Troy right there with him, wanted to keep on running, to topple over the cliff together.

"Keep doing that," Troy said between grunts. He started to speak again, but it came out garbled as he continued to ride Finn, as Finn teetered right on the edge of completely losing it. Then Troy cursed and moaned and came all over Finn's chest. Troy was so fucking beautiful as he lost it. Finn felt warmth rising up his chest, all of his feelings for Troy, the lust and love and everything, swirling together and making his head spin. Troy's body clamped down on Finn's cock, and the extra pressure and vibration was all Finn needed to topple over the cliff. He grabbed Troy's hips, thrust up once more, and came, jerking as the convulsions ripped through him. He cried out Troy's name.

They collapsed in a heap on the bed. They lay silent and panting, tangled up in each other. After a while, Troy said, "That was so fucking good."

"Oh yeah."

He leaned over and gave Finn a sloppy kiss. Troy pulled away slightly and settled half on top of Finn, his head resting on Finn's chest. He put his hands on either side of Finn's torso. His chest rose and fell against Finn's skin.

"Finn?"

"Yeah?"

Troy didn't say anything. Finn was starting to get itchy and wanted to go clean up, but Troy's silence bothered him. "Troy, what is it?"

"I, um." He propped himself up on his hands and looked down at Finn. His facial expression was surprising: eyebrows knit together with worry, lips pursed. "I know there's not, like, a relationship playbook, and even if there were, we sure as hell haven't followed it."

"Uh-huh."

"I just wanted to say… I don't know. Being with you is kind of a weird thing. This was not really gentle lovemaking, you know?"

Finn found that confusing. "Is that what you want?"

Troy looked away. "I'm not sure."

Finn ran a hand across Troy's shoulders. "Here's what I think. I think sex with you is fun and exciting, and I always want to do it again as soon as we're done. I may never get enough of you is how I feel sometimes. And that can only be a good thing. Who cares if it's rough or gentle or vanilla or kinky as long as it's good?"

Troy laughed softly and settled his head back down on Finn's chest. "Mmm, yes, I agree. Have you always felt that way about me?"

"Yeah, I guess so."

"Then why were you always running away?"

"Come on. You know why. Everything I feel for you is

so messy and confusing. I was really pissed at you, genuinely so, for a really long time. It disturbed me that my desire for you was so insatiable. And I guess I panicked. You made me feel things no one ever made me feel, and it confused me that we fought so much but were still so sexually compatible, and I just don't know. And it's not… it's not just sex, you know? With you, it has never been just about sex."

"You're not going to run away now, are you?"

"This is my apartment. Where would I go?"

"I meant figuratively. If you start to freak out again, are you going to bail on us?"

Finn didn't know. He still wasn't sure any of this was real. It was so difficult to reconcile those old resentments with what he was feeling now. "Can we table this for now?"

"Yeah." Troy moved away from Finn and lay on his back. "The ghost thing?"

"Until I can be sure…"

"Say no more. Discussion tabled."

Finn got up and went into the bathroom, where he cleaned up. When he came back into his bedroom, Troy was curled up on his side, staring unfocused at something near Finn's dresser. "I'm sorry," said Finn.

"I wish you'd trust your feelings more. Trust the things you feel when we're together. I believe you when you say you were mad at me for a long time, but I don't think you are anymore, and it's time to stop pretending things are the way they used to be. Even if the ghosts nudged us toward each other, I can't believe that everything that's happened over the last few weeks is a lie."

"I thought we were tabling this discussion."

"I love you, Finn. More than I've ever loved anyone."

Finn wished Troy would stop saying things like that. Finn felt it too, but he wasn't ready to talk about it yet.

He grunted and rolled over so that his back was to Finn. "All right, I'm done."

Finn lay back down on the bed. He moved the sheets around, and then pulled them up to cover his and Troy's bodies. He put an arm around Troy's waist and spooned up behind him. "None of this makes any sense."

"Who said love had to make any sense? As far as I can tell, love is completely nonsensical. That's sort of the beauty of it."

Finn pressed his face into Troy's back. He didn't want to talk about it anymore. Troy was upset now. Finn could tell by the set of his shoulders, the way his jaw clenched, but Finn couldn't figure out how to make it better, so he just lay there, holding Troy. Eventually, they both drifted off to sleep.

Chapter 19

Finn and Troy emerged from the subway to a gray sky.

"Wasn't it sunny when we left?" Finn asked.

Troy had been watching the weather all day, hoping it would stay sunny for their walk through the cemetery. He found cemeteries especially macabre when it was raining. He tried to stay optimistic. "It's been like this all day, sunny one minute and cloudy the next. I'm sure we'll be fine."

They walked quickly up the hill to Green-Wood Cemetery. Troy had drawn a crude map showing approximately where Brill and Cutler were buried according to records he'd found online. Finn was far more familiar with the cemetery's layout, so Troy handed him the map as they walked through the main gate.

Finn led the way, and after about ten minutes of walking—with Finn stopping to point out the graves of various famous New Yorkers—they came across the Brill plot.

"This is interesting," Troy said, taking in the group of graves as a whole. There were seventeen graves marked "Brill" in a small area belonging to patriarch Augustus Brill, his children, and their spouses. Theodore Cummings Brill was buried there, but off to the side, which struck Troy as symbolic. His family must have known about his being gay, about the relationship with Cutler, all of it.

"It's a damn shame he and Cutler weren't buried together," Finn said.

"It's not like they're really here."

"I know, but…it would have been the right thing to do. Just like Brill's siblings were all buried with their spouses."

Troy gave Finn a long look and had a fleeting thought about a relationship like that with him—something about the word "spouse" caught him off guard—but he filed it away for later.

He looked at the grave and was struck suddenly by the realness of it. There was something so remote about the subjects of his research sometimes, and the nature of this particular investigation made Brill seem even more like part of a dream. But here was proof he existed. Here was his final resting place. His very body was under the earth, marked with a simple headstone bearing only his name and the years he lived, 1842–1878.

"He was only two years older than I am now," Troy said.

Finn ran a warm hand up Troy's arm. Troy found it comforting.

"It's a real tragedy that they died so young. I feel like I knew them, you know?" said Finn. "And the closer I get to the end of Cutler's journal, the more I dread what's coming. Is that weird?"

"No. I feel the same way." There was a distant roar of sound that Troy thought must have been thunder. "Come on, let's find Cutler."

George Washington Cutler was buried a fair distance from Brill. Their funerals had been held on different days. The Brills had made a public showing of being horrified by the sudden death of their son, but Brill's journal indicated they were barely in touch toward the end of his life. Troy was now certain the estrangement had been borne of a specific incident, one Brill often referred to but never described. Of course, Brill had probably been happier not under the thumb of his parents, who kept tight control over the other

Brill children throughout their lives.

Cutler's grave was by itself, no family nearby. Troy had dug up the records which indicated that Cutler had almost no family left in New York when he died, save for an uncle. The funeral and headstone had been paid for with the money Cutler left behind. Thus he had quite a nice plot, on a hill near the grave of Charles Ebbets, of Brooklyn Dodgers fame. Troy studied the marker for a long time. It was similar to Brill's, bearing only his name and the years he lived—he'd been born in 1840.

"I don't suppose anyone leaves flowers out for the long dead," said Troy.

"Well, you'd be surprised. Less so these days, but some of the more famous residents here get wreaths or bouquets when their birthdays or death anniversaries roll around. I was here a few years ago on Leonard Bernstein's birthday, and his whole headstone was covered in flowers. Granted, it's not very big, it's a 'blink and you'll miss it' stone up on the hill there." Finn pointed. "But still."

"Point taken, but Bernstein hasn't been dead that long. There are plenty of people still alive who knew him well." Troy contemplated the stone. "I wish we'd thought to bring flowers."

"Next time."

There was another rumble of thunder. Troy looked at the sky and felt uneasy. "Maybe we should move on."

Finn nodded in agreement and led Troy back down the hill. Finn had asked if they could swing by his family plot, which was apparently something of a tradition whenever he came to Green-Wood, and Troy had agreed, but now the skies were making him nervous.

"You know where you're going, right?" said Troy.

"The Finnegan plot is probably a five-minute walk from here. Sort of to the west."

"Let's go. I want to get back on the train before it starts raining."

Finn led the way down pathways and over hills until Troy felt utterly lost. He'd always liked Green-Wood, but all the business with ghosts lately made him a little nervous about being in a cemetery. Now that Troy knew ghosts were real, he concluded this cemetery was probably full of them, under his feet, in the mausoleums, all around.

A large raindrop landed on Troy's nose. "Uh, Finn…"

"I know, I felt it too. Just a little drizzle. The plot is over this way."

He knew it was in his head, but he kept thinking that the angels and statues that stood atop various grave markers were moving to watch their progress. Finn seemed oblivious and of singular purpose, until they arrived at a fork in the path.

"I think it's that way," Finn said, pointing to one side of the fork, which looked identical to the other. Then he plodded down the path.

Troy trailed after him, looking around. He fumbled with the printed cemetery map, but he was so lost that he wasn't sure what he was looking for. That the cemetery seemed completely empty of other people was unnerving too. Granted, Green-Wood didn't typically get a lot of visitors on weekdays, but it freaked him out that there were no other people at all.

"Oh, here's Boss Tweed," Finn said, stopping. Troy stood beside him and gazed at the Tweed family markers. "I considered writing my dissertation on Tammany Hall."

"I understand that he was quite the ladies' man, despite his corpulence," said Troy, trying to keep the unease out of his voice. "He was kind of a bear, if that's your thing."

Finn nodded and then looked at Troy. His brow furrowed. "Are you okay?"

"Fine."

"Are you cold? You're shaking."

"Fine, just, you know, overcast skies plus cemetery. I sort of gave myself the heebie-jeebies."

Finn rubbed Troy's back. Then he turned. "Let's keep moving," he said.

Eventually, Finn stepped off the path. Troy followed him, dodging graves. He'd always thought it was inappropriate to step on the place where someone was buried, but, given the density of markers in the cemetery, it couldn't be helped. He half expected a hand to reach out of the ground and grab his foot.

Finn stopped in front of a small collection of graves, all of which bore the name Finnegan. "Robert and Beatrice were my grandparents," Finn said, motioning toward their markers. "There's a Christopher Finnegan here too. He was my uncle. Died in Vietnam. I'm named for him." He pointed to the plain, military marker with the cross carved into the stone. "It's why I started going by Finn. Christopher was my dad's dead brother." He took a deep breath. "The stones on the left are a little older." He walked forward and squinted at the names carved on a few more modest stones. "My great-great grandparents are buried here too. They were the generation after we immigrated."

"Interesting. Would any of your family have lived in Brooklyn?"

"No. My grandparents were still in the Lower East Side as kids but moved to Queens when they got married. And my parents live in Connecticut now, so…"

"I was just curious if our ancestors had run into each other. If, say, my great grandfather might have run into some old aunt of yours and been instantly smitten."

Finn smirked. "Well, I guess that is not so difficult to picture. Just as well that they didn't, though. That would make our relationship weird and incestual."

Troy was in the process of leaning over to kiss the smirk right off Finn's face when there was a clap of thunder. He straightened again and looked up. The sky had turned an ominous shade of green. "That can't be good."

"Let's get out of here."

They jogged back the way they came. Troy's sense that doom was imminent grew as they moved. Even if zombies didn't rise out of the graves—which was up there on Troy's list of secret fears—it looked like they were about to get caught in one hell of a thunderstorm.

He fretted and didn't pay particular attention as they ran until Finn stopped abruptly and shouted, "Fuck. I think we're lost."

"Lost? How can we be lost? All we had to do was go back the way we came."

"I know! I thought that's where we were going. I must have made a wrong turn somewhere. I don't know where we are now." He turned in a circle, his gaze passing over grave markers.

Troy felt a big rain drop hit the top of his head. "Okay, the street is over there. I can see a fast-food joint and a bank on the other side of the fence. Can we just follow the fence until we get to the main gate again?"

Finn's face was a picture of panic, his eyes wide, his eyebrows raised. Raindrops pelted them, dampening and darkening the blond curls on Finn's head. "Yeah, I guess that's one way to do it. It'll take longer, though. The cemetery has a perimeter of several miles. If we go the wrong way, it'll take us all afternoon to get back. There's an entrance nearby, but it's usually locked. It'll take less time to go to the one I know is open."

"Oh."

Troy pulled out his map, but it wasn't that helpful because he wasn't exactly sure where he was in the cemetery. It was a huge space, and all of the paths looked the same. He jogged to where the nearest paths intersected, looking for signs.

Finn grunted. "Well, we came from that way, so let's try turning over there and see where it gets us. I've spent a fair amount of time in this cemetery. If I can find a landmark, I should be able to get us back."

"Okay."

The rain picked up as Finn and Troy jogged again. Nothing looked familiar to Troy. The grave markers all started to look the same. Miles and miles of granite spires and angels and monoliths. Rain fell faster. The drops stuck to Troy's glasses. He pulled them off his face and shoved them in his pocket, finding his un-aided, hazy vision slightly better than trying to see through rain-speckled lenses. This plan worked fine until Finn stopped abruptly again. Troy's depth perception was off without his glasses, and he stumbled into Finn. If Finn hadn't reached out and caught him, they might have both landed on what was now a muddy grave.

Thunder roared and lightning flashed all around the

cemetery. Rain fell in sheets. Troy wished with everything he had that they could get out of the cemetery.

"This is a lost cause!" Finn shouted. "There's a mausoleum over there. Let's go in and wait out the storm."

Troy ran after Finn, who ducked under the mausoleum door's overhang. The mausoleum itself was ostentatious and overwrought, in Troy's opinion, with two rows of Doric columns leading to a ten-foot-tall entrance. There was a lock on the door, but they both fit under the overhang, and it was enough to keep them sheltered.

"Fat lot of good that did. I'm already soaked," said Troy.

"What happened to your glasses?"

Troy pulled them out of his pocket. "It was easier to see without them." He slid them on and pointed to the streaks of rain to demonstrate. Still unable to see through the lenses and not seeing anything dry enough to wipe them with, he took them off again. It took him a moment to realize Finn was staring.

"What?"

"Your eyes are really weird. Blue with green specs. I never noticed before."

"I don't know if I should take that as a compliment." Troy slid his glasses back into his pocket. "Surely you've spent a little bit of time gazing into my eyes. You've seen me without my glasses on before."

"It is a compliment. Usually, when I'm looking at you, you have your glasses on, or I'm looking at…other things." Finn cleared his throat. "But I like your eyes. I…"

Finn trailed off, so Troy took the opportunity to kiss him. The rain continue to fall around them, and there was a crack of thunder in the distance, but it didn't matter because Finn's mouth was hot and enthusiastic against his own. He pressed his hand against the small of Finn's back and felt Finn's wet T-shirt and the heat of his skin beneath it.

They eased apart, and Finn laughed. "I don't think I can make out with you with this many dead people around."

"Fair point." Troy looked up at mausoleum door. BEAUCHAMP. "Hey, that name we ran across in both journals." He pointed to the name above the door.

"Huh," said Finn. "That's weird. I wonder who's buried here."

"Need I remind you that the door is locked?"

Finn pulled a Swiss army knife out of his pocket. He fiddled with the lock for a long moment before it clicked. The door groaned as Finn pulled it open.

"Wow!" said Troy. "I'll have to add lock picking to your considerable list of skills."

Finn raised an eyebrow at Troy. "It was an old lock, pretty easy to jimmy. What other things are on this list?"

"Oh, you know. Research, logical thinking, pick-up basketball, blowjobs, those sorts of things."

"Thanks, I think." Finn went inside the vault.

"So you are of the criminal element now. No wonder you didn't finish your PhD."

Finn turned around and glared. "Shut up, Troy."

"Sorry. Low blow." Troy rocked on his heels. "So who's interred here?"

There was a wall of coffin-sized lockers, each with a plaque displaying a name and a set of years. Troy scanned the names until he settled on one that looked interesting.

"Here we go. Nicholas Beauchamp. Born 1845, died 1904."

"Okay. But we don't know anything about this guy. It might not even be the same Mr. Beauchamp."

"No, but we have a name to look up."

"There's no way it's that easy."

"Hey, maybe it's nothing. Maybe this Nicholas Beauchamp lived on Staten Island and never met Brill or Cutler and has nothing to do with this mystery at all. Maybe he was a friend of Cutler's but doesn't play into the murder. Maybe he's the killer. Anything is possible. I mean, after everything we've seen the last few weeks, even you have to admit that this could be related somehow."

"Yeah, yeah."

Troy pulled his wallet out and searched it for something to write on. "You have a pen?" he asked Finn.

"I think so." Finn pulled a pen from his pocket.

Troy found a receipt and scribbled down "Nicholas Beauchamp" and his lifespan. He tucked the receipt back into his wallet. He handed the pen back to Finn.

"You keep a condom in your wallet?" Finn said. "Isn't that a little high school?"

"Hey, it never hurts to be prepared."

"Just so you know, I'm not having sex with you in a mausoleum."

"I didn't ask you to. That's gross."

"Okay, just checking." Finn walked back to the door and peered outside. "Hey, come take a look at this."

Troy stepped toward Finn. The sky was blue and the sun shone brightly. "What the hell?"

"I think that's Beecher's grave over there." Finn went

outside.

Troy pulled the door of the mausoleum closed, and it locked again with a clang. He trailed after Finn, who stopped in front of a statue of Henry Ward Beecher.

"How did we come to be on top of a hill?" Troy asked, looking around.

"I don't know." Finn looked at the grave marker. "Everything got confusing when it started raining. I know where we are now, though. The entrance is over that way." He pointed. "Let's get the hell out of here."

Chapter 20

Troy took the stairs up to the second floor of the Brill house, where he found Finn contemplating the bed in Brill's former chamber. "I've got some info on Beauchamp," Troy said.

Finn nodded.

Troy handed over his notes. "From what I can tell, Beauchamp enlisted in the Union army on his eighteenth birthday in 1863 and then settled in Brooklyn after the war. I can't find an address, but it seems possible that he and Brill could have been neighbors."

"It could be a giant coincidence," Finn said, looking over the notes.

"You're right, it could be. Although I don't know if I believe in coincidence anymore."

Finn turned and raised an eyebrow.

"Before you yell at me, would you please take five seconds to entertain the possibility that Brill or Cutler knew Nicholas Beauchamp and that he's involved in the murder somehow?"

"Even if I do, I don't know what this proves." Finn's shoulders were slumped. He handed the notes back to Troy, and he turned to look at the bed again. Troy couldn't figure out what Finn was doing in the room. He'd said twenty minutes before that he wanted to see something in the master bedroom.

"Maybe it doesn't prove anything," Troy said. "I intend to keep digging, though. We've got another year or so of journal entries to go through, right? I'm supposed to get the last volume of Brill's back from the lab tomorrow. Maybe

Beauchamp will turn up again. Maybe he'll be a red herring like Rawley was, someone who gets mentioned once in the journals and then never again. But maybe he's involved in all this somehow. I don't see the usefulness in discounting any possibility just because you're so goddamn determined to think all of it is ridiculous."

"I never said that."

"What are you even doing here anyway?"

"This bed is new to the bedroom. It's not Brill and Cutler's bed."

"That's correct, as far as I know." Troy wondered what Finn was getting at. "I'm pretty sure this one came from the KCHS's collection of antique furniture. I could check on its origins if you really want. I've got all of the information in a file downstairs."

"Cutler wrote an entry about how he had his tools up here and was using them to repair a broken hinge on the door of Brill's armoire. Something startled him, and he wound up sort of tossing his hammer. He wrote that the action put a nick in one of the posts. There's no nick here, though. Not the same bed."

"Oh." Troy frowned.

"Cutler was a carpenter. He was good with tools."

"Right." Troy collected his thoughts. "So this is a different bed. Most of the furniture in the house came from other places. Except for the chaise, obviously."

"Ah, the fucking chaise, of course. Another coincidence."

"Well, if you're going to stand here contemplating the furniture, I'm going to go back downstairs and see what else I can find on Beauchamp."

"Have fun."

Troy bristled at Finn's sarcasm. His anger kicked up a notch, so he took a deep breath to try to calm down. "Look, a healthy amount of skepticism is good for an investigation like this. But so is an open mind. I wouldn't be too quick to judge. That's all I'm saying."

"So, fine. All this furniture came from some other mystery place, this bed belonged to some other person, but the chaise magically stayed in the house through many owners and generations. That kind of coincidence is not really out of the realm of possibility, so I'll go with it. But I'm supposed to think that the ghosts steered us toward a random mausoleum in the middle of a cemetery in order to give us a clue? It's hard enough to accept that the ghosts have been moving objects in this building, and that they've also infected my mind enough to give me dreams, but now this? It's all too much. I don't know if I can do this anymore."

"Come on, Finn."

"No, you come on! I'm tired of being manipulated, and I'm tired of dead ends, and I'm tired of goddamn gay ghosts. None of this matters! Even if we solve the murder, it's not like any justice can be served, because the murderer must have died more than a hundred years ago."

"But the ghosts…"

"Fuck the ghosts!"

The air in the room changed abruptly as if to mirror Finn's angry mood. While Finn continued to shout at Troy, Troy started to tune him out, distracted now by the way the wind swirled and caught the curtains, the way the lights dimmed. Finn didn't seem to notice, still caught up in his rant.

"Finn, shut up a minute."

"What? How dare you——" He shut his mouth and looked around the room. "Holy shit," he muttered.

"I think it's safe to say that someone is trying to tell us something. Maybe we're going down the wrong path."

"Wrong path, my ass. This whole thing is a wild-goose chase. You thought they committed suicide, remember? So, fine, I'm willing to buy they were murdered, but how the fuck would we ever find their murderers? Not to mention that——"

In a flash, Finn's body lifted off the ground and was thrown against the wall. He gasped. His head slammed back too. He collapsed in a heap on the floor.

"Finn! Jesus Christ." Troy ran to his side. "Are you okay?" Finn clearly wasn't, because his eyes were closed and his whole body had gone slack. "Don't you dare be seriously injured." Troy maneuvered Finn's body a little. He felt for breath and a pulse, then sighed in relief; Finn had just been knocked unconscious. To the ghosts, he said, "I hope you're happy. He's not going to be able to help you if he's badly hurt."

All activity in the room stopped. The wind stilled, the curtains fell against the windows, and the lights went up to full brightness. Troy thought he could even feel contrition. He pulled out his phone and dialed 911.

When the ambulance came, Troy told the paramedics that Finn had tripped over something and fallen against the wall. They let him ride along with Finn to the hospital, but things got a little hairy when they brought Finn into the ER. A nurse stopped Troy and told him he couldn't go into the examination room.

Troy grunted. "Can I just… I mean, I need to know he's okay. He's my boyfriend."

The nurse nodded and at least looked sympathetic.

"I'll come get you as soon as he's awake."

* * *

Finn woke up in a hospital. Or at least, that was his first conclusion. Stale antiseptic smell, white walls, weird-looking equipment. And he was in the room alone. It required some work and heavy breathing not to panic. How on earth had he ended up in the hospital? And why did his head feel like someone had driven a freight train over it? He waited a minute to see if someone would show up. Then he found a call button.

A nurse popped her head into the room. "Oh, you're awake."

"What happened? Why am I here? A minute ago, I was fighting with Troy, and now I'm in the hospital?"

"Are you in pain?"

"Yeah, my head hurts like hell."

The nurse walked over. "You have a concussion. We're keeping you overnight to make sure there's no more severe damage, but the fact that you're conscious and alert now is a good sign. I'll check with the doctor about getting you some pain meds."

"Thanks. Now what happened?"

The nurse eyed him warily. "It seems you fell and hit your head. At least, that's what your boyfriend said."

"My boyfriend? Oh, Troy. Okay. Where is he?"

"He didn't push you, did he?"

Did he? No, Troy had been standing on the other side of the room. But he did remember getting pushed. How was that possible? No one had been in the room with them. Well, no one except the fucking ghosts. "No, he didn't. I know he looks strong, but he couldn't hurt a fly. I must have tripped. Is he here?"

"I've seen domestic abuse cases in gay couples before. It's nothing to be ashamed of. I can get a counselor to come talk to you, if you like."

Finn's brain wasn't firing on all cylinders and, in fact, his head was getting foggier by the minute, so he was having a difficult time processing what the nurse was saying. "Domestic abuse?" He grunted. "No, that's not… Troy has never touched me unless I wanted him to, okay? He didn't push me. There's no abuse. Now, please, is he in the hospital? I'd like to talk to him."

Finn half expected the nurse to say Troy had gone home. That would probably go a ways toward convincing her Troy was a deadbeat boyfriend-abuser.

Instead she nodded. "Yes, he's in the waiting room. I'll go get him."

She came back a minute later with Troy in tow. Troy approached the bed and stood there, fiddling with the watch on his left wrist. The nurse hovered in the door.

"Can we have a minute?" Troy asked her.

She hesitated. "All right." She looked at Finn and added, "I'll be right outside. You push the button if you need anything."

Troy looked puzzled when Finn focused his attention back on him. "She thinks you beat me up," Finn said.

"Ah, that explains the open hostility. Here I thought she found my Tom Ford tie offensive." He ran a hand over it. The tie was a slightly crazy purple and black herringbone. Finn found he had to look away from it to keep from getting dizzy. "How are you?"

"Sore. What happened?"

"You were shouting at me and you know who, and I think one of them took umbrage at your skepticism. Before I knew what was happening, you'd been thrown against the wall and knocked unconscious."

"The nurse said I have a concussion."

"Yeah, I saw you hit your head. She told me they were keeping you overnight."

"Uh-huh. So you told them you were my boyfriend." Something about that didn't sit right with Finn. The sound of the word was wrong to his ears. Sure, they'd been kind of dating, but he didn't really think of Troy as his boyfriend. Not yet.

"I had to make a snap decision, and I thought that increased the odds I'd get to see you when you woke up."

Finn rubbed his forehead, trying to stay focused. His head pounded. "You have a lot more faith in the system than I do. If you'd said brother, okay. Good friend, even. But boyfriend? You're lucky they didn't light you on fire."

"They don't burn queers anymore, Finn. This is Brooklyn in the twenty-first century. Besides, I didn't have much time to think it through. The word just kind of came out of my mouth."

"You're not my boyfriend."

"Thanks, Finn. I love you too."

Finn rolled his eyes, which hurt a whole lot. He coughed and then groaned at the pain. Troy reached over and eased him back onto the pillows, which was a very boyfriend-like thing to do. Finn let his head sink back. "I don't know what we are," he said. "We've known each other for years, and we fuck sometimes, but that does not make us boyfriends."

Troy's face seemed to darken, his brow creased, his eyes a little angry, a frown forming on his lips. "Fine, I'm not your boyfriend. You've made yourself very clear on that front." He looked away. "I guess this means the honeymoon is over. Have the ghosts given up on you?"

"What do you mean?" He noticed suddenly that Troy looked hurt. That wasn't what Finn expected. Angry, sure, but hurt? Finn tried to think through what Troy had just said. Were the ghosts done with him? He was kind of done with the ghosts, patience-wise. He was tired of the investigation, yes, sick of the nonsense with the ghosts, and now he'd landed in the hospital with a concussion, and he was *pissed*. More at the ghosts than at Troy.

Troy whispered, "I just thought maybe you'd finally succeeded in getting the ghosts out of your head, so you don't care about me anymore."

Which wasn't true at all, as far as Finn could tell. He didn't know if the ghosts were still hovering around, but he still had feelings for Troy, despite his anger. "I'm sorry. I shouldn't have taken my rage out on you."

Troy looked at him, his brows knit together. "That's all you have to say?"

"I don't know what you want from me, Troy. I don't know what to call this...relationship between us. I mean, yes, I have feelings for you, okay? I like you. I care about you. Maybe I even love you. But I hadn't thought of us as boyfriends. The word surprised me, is all."

Troy closed his eyes for a long moment. "Fine."

"My head hurts too much to have this conversation right now. Let's talk later."

"Yes, that's fine."

Troy's curt tone bothered Finn, but he knew when to back off. Instead, he reached over and took Troy's hand. "Thank you for staying."

"Of course."

"I hate hospitals."

"Is that why you're so ornery?"

"I had appendicitis when I was fifteen. They had to do emergency surgery. The hospital was especially crowded that day, though, so I had to share a room with some old man. I'd had a mild allergic reaction to the anesthetic, so they kept me there a couple of days to make sure there weren't any other complications from surgery, and I was so out of it that I slept most of the time anyway. When I woke up the last morning, the old man was dead."

"Oh, God. That's awful."

"I'm glad that other bed is empty. I keep thinking they're going to wheel in an old man."

Troy shook his head. "There are still so many things about you I never knew."

Finn shrugged. "I'm sure the reverse is true too. Look, I'm sorry for yelling, and I'm sorry I upset you. But this is all very new and weird for me. And at this point, I mostly want to solve the mystery so that I can get on with my life. And if you're a part of that life, then so be it."

Troy smirked. "I see the light of your affection for me remains undimmed."

"Truce?"

"Yeah, truce." Troy bent his head and leaned his forehead against Finn's. Finn found some comfort in their proximity. He squeezed Troy's hand. Troy moved his head slightly and gave Finn a series of soft kisses. Things were just starting to get good when someone cleared her throat.

Troy backed up and turned around. "Ah, Nurse Ratched."

"Ha, ha," said the nurse coming back into the room. She checked the machines attached to Finn, and then said to Troy, "Mr. Finnegan needs his rest."

"Okay. I'll pick you up tomorrow. Sleep well."

"Night, Troy." It occurred to Finn that this would be a good opportunity to deploy the L-word. Wasn't that how couples said good-bye to each other? Although, hadn't he just finished explaining to Troy that they weren't a couple? The look of longing on Troy's face almost made him throw all that out the window, but he took a deep breath and stuck to his principles.

Troy nodded and gave a little wave, then left the room.

Chapter 21

While he was in the hospital, Finn's dreams were wonderfully bland. No top hats or waistcoats or wispy sideburns. No ghosts or hauntings.

So it stood to reason that once he was home, after Troy and Janice had put him to bed and gone back into the living room to conspire, he had a real doozy of a dream.

It took him a moment to realize he was looking in a mirror. He didn't recognize the face staring back at him until he moved and realized he was gazing at George Washington Cutler. He ran a hand over his goatee, the texture both new and familiar.

Finn considered the image in the mirror. A thousand thoughts about Cutler flew through his head, but he wasn't sure how much of it he knew because he was researching the man or how much he knew because he was in Wash's head.

Since coming to live with Teddy, he'd put on a little weight and made an effort to improve his appearance, but was extremely self-conscious. He wanted to be thought of as handsome but not as a dandy, which would be too much of a giveaway. His primary motivation was that he wanted other men—Teddy especially, but men generally also—to find him handsome and attractive. He therefore started bathing more often, and he carefully combed his hair every morning and groomed the goatee and used a salve on his skin to keep it smooth.

He had the rugged body of a man who'd been born to a working-class family. He'd seen action in a few places during the war as well. He'd come home with an injured ankle and a tendency toward nightmares. After the war, he went to work as a carpenter for his uncle who owned a furniture shop on Montague Street in Brooklyn, a few blocks from the Brill House. The chaise longue in the parlor had been Wash's handiwork.

The only real negative of working for his uncle was that he was nagged fairly regularly about his bachelor status. He'd been engaged to a woman named Adele, the daughter of a friend of his mother. Adele was pretty enough, but Wash didn't feel any kind of pull toward her, not like the pull he found to some of the men in his employ, not the same lust he would come to feel for Teddy. She'd died suddenly of influenza about six weeks before the wedding. Her death was a continued source of shame for Wash, both because he'd felt more relieved by it than anything else, but also because he continued to use his obligatory mourning as his excuse not to get married.

This was information Finn had instantly as he looked at his reflection. It wasn't background he'd gleaned from the journal—the details of his war service, his engagement to Adele—none of that had been committed to paper. He just knew everything there was to know about George Washington Cutler in the instant he met the man's eyes in the mirror.

He looked at the reflection and wasted a minute wondering at the futility of wearing a suit to a job where he was likely to get it dirty. The suit was a fine gray tweed, sturdy enough for the fall weather. He ran his hands over the lapels. Then he turned to find his hat.

Teddy stood in the doorway to their bedroom. "Off to the shop?"

"Yes. My cousin John is sick, so I should go early. A woman in Gravesend put in an order for a dozen chairs. She needs them for some dinner party next Thursday."

Teddy smiled. The smile threw Wash—and Finn, frankly—off track. Finn smiled back. It was so gloriously mundane, speaking just about work, nothing loaded about their conversation, just everyday things.

"What are your plans for today?" asked Finn.

"I have not decided. I am supposed to meet with some friend of my father's for lunch. I am not entirely sure what we are to discuss. Some kind of business venture, I take it. I didn't have the heart to tell him I have no money to invest in a business." He looked out the window.

Wash took a step closer. "I have money enough to contribute. I could go back to paying you some kind of monthly rent."

"What, for your half of the bed? No, I could not think of charging you for your company."

Finn thought Teddy had a point. Given the circumstances, Wash paying rent felt a little like paying for sex.

Having that thought somehow triggered a whole wave of images from the recesses of Wash's memory, most of them flashes of erotic moments between Teddy and Wash. Finn found himself gasping, not ready for the onslaught.

"Are you all right?" Teddy asked.

"Yes, fine," said Finn. He found himself laughing. "I was just thinking about something…"

As if they were sharing the same psychic space, Teddy's face changed suddenly. There was lust in his eyes, heat evident on his face.

Then they were on each other frantically, kissing with more passion than Finn thought he'd ever felt, everything rising up and crashing like waves. Finn worried someone would see them since the door was open, but the next thought answered his question—no one could see inside Teddy's bedroom from the stairwell, and besides, the tenants never came to the second floor, meaning Teddy's quarters were completely private.

Finn extracted himself, aware that he had to go to work and that if he and Teddy got too carried away he'd have to do the whole morning beauty routine again. He ran his hands over his hair.

"You look handsome as always," Teddy said, smoothing down Wash's lapels.

"You don't think I am too fussy?"

"Of course not, darling."

"I worry I…" Finn held up his arm and dropped his wrist, a gesture he figured would probably be lost on a gentleman of the 1870s. "I do not wish to be perceived as a…you know. A Miss Nancy." Finn almost laughed when the words came out of his mouth. He loved the Victorian slang for "gay."

Teddy rested his hands on Wash's shoulders. "You are about the most masculine man I have ever met. You like fashionable things, yes, but I do not think anyone would mistake you for anything other than an attractive man who likes nice clothes. You're not advertising anything."

"Teddy, I…" Finn could feel the turmoil in Wash, his conflicting desire to look good for Teddy, and his fear of being picked out as a homosexual. He frowned. "I am a nance," he whispered.

Teddy leaned over and kissed his cheek. "Maybe so, but no one need know that save you and I."

Finn liked the smell of the other man, and he leaned in closer to get a better sense of it. He wished he had time to explore his attraction. Instead, he settled for nipping at Teddy's lip, which earned him a tender kiss and a tight hug.

"Have a good day, Wash. I love you."

It was so sweet it was heartbreaking. Finn closed his eyes and put his arms around Teddy. "I love you."

In a flash, he was in the shop. He sat in front of a chair, completing finishing touches on the scrollwork. It was incredible to be in Wash's body for the moment. Finn knew basically nothing about woodwork, but his hands—Wash's hands—were producing something truly beautiful. How had he not known sooner that Wash was so gifted?

His uncle, a man named Elijah Fenton, came into the room and reminded Wash that they needed all of the chairs done by Tuesday so they could be delivered to Mrs. Arlington in time. Wash went through some mental calculations for how many hours of work remained ahead of him to get everything ready. He lamented the extra hours he'd have to work—hours spent away from Teddy—and Finn sympathized.

Then Fenton said, "Mrs. Fenton made the acquaintance of a lovely young woman recently. I was told to pass along to you that Mrs. Fenton would like to have you over for dinner next week, after the Arlington project is done. She intends for me to tell you that this is purely to thank you for your good work recently, but naturally, she wants you to meet this woman. Her name is…Sophia, I think. Clayton Embry's daughter."

Wash put a considerable effort into not rolling his eyes. "I'm sure Sophia Embry is lovely, but I am not very interested in courting a woman right now."

"Why not? Do not tell me it is because you still pine away for Adele. So much time has gone by. I barely remember what she looks like."

Wash couldn't remember either. He sometimes closed his eyes and tried to picture her, but nothing would appear besides blonde ringlets framing a blurry face. He had Teddy's whole appearance committed to memory, however, and could summon his image with barely any effort. "It's not that," he said. "I mean, I'm busy here, of course, and I—"

Fenton laughed. "You're courting someone else, aren't you?"

Wash bristled. "What makes you say that?"

"You've had a lighter step these last few months. In my experience, there is only one thing that can do that to a man."

Wash felt trapped. "I assure you, I am not courting a woman."

Fenton clucked his tongue. "Of course. So you will come to dinner."

"I—"

The conversation was stalled by a customer coming into the store. Fenton walked up to the front to take care of him. Wash went back to his chair.

When Finn woke up, he heard voices in the living room. He looked around his bedroom. The bed felt empty, and the half beside him was rumpled, like there had been someone there who had since departed. That was disappointing; he wished Troy were with him. It still felt a little odd to want such a thing, but he tried not to talk himself out of it. He got out of bed and walked toward the voices. He found Troy—

wearing a T-shirt and wrinkled yoga pants—and Janice, chatting on the living room couch.

"What time is it?" Finn asked.

Troy glanced at the wall clock. "Uh. One-thirty. In the morning."

Finn nodded.

"Did you need something?" Troy asked.

"A glass of water?"

"Sure. Sit down. You should still be in bed."

"I woke up."

Janice walked into the kitchen while Troy coaxed Finn onto the couch. She returned with the glass.

"I had a dream."

Troy tilted his head. He put an arm behind Finn on the couch. Wanting to feel the warmth from Troy's body, desiring more than anything the emotional closeness he'd felt to Teddy in his dream, he leaned against Troy. When he finished his water, he put the glass on the coffee table. He leaned back and put his head on Troy's shoulder. Troy hugged Finn tighter to him.

Finn related the dream. Troy and Janice occasionally interrupted to ask questions. He concluded by saying, "These dreams are always vivid, but they're strange because sometimes I have free will and sometimes I really don't."

"Was there anything threatening in the dream?" asked Troy.

"No. I don't know that this dream sheds any light on the mystery, and that's assuming that what we're seeing are Brill and Cutler's memories and not just our own brains working overtime."

"You should probably go back to bed, Mr. Concussion," Janice said. Finn had told her some of what had happened with the case so far, but he supposed having dreams as Cutler made him sound a little crazy.

"Yeah, yeah." To Troy, Finn said, "Will you come with me?"

"All right, but no funny business. You should sleep. You're not even supposed to be out of bed."

"I feel okay. Really."

Troy stood and helped Finn up. Janice kept shooting him raised-eyebrow looks. He didn't have the energy to get into any kind of explanation for why his feud with Troy was over, or why they'd been sleeping together regularly, or even why he really just wanted to lie in bed with Troy for a while. So he simply said, "Night, Janice."

Troy steered him back to his room and eased him down onto the bed. Then he pulled off his T-shirt and climbed in beside Finn. He pulled the sheets up over their bodies. "How are you, really?"

"I do feel much better. I just… Come here." Finn snuggled up against him. Then there it was: the connection. Troy put his arms around Finn. Troy's skin was warm against him. Their hearts beat against each other. This was a man who understood him, who cared about him, who loved him. He returned that love, even if he hadn't said the words yet, and hoped to continue to return it for as long as he was able. If that meant just the duration of their investigation, so be it, because he at least got this taste.

Troy kissed the top of his head. "Sweet dreams, darling."

Finn didn't respond. He closed his eyes, laid his head against Troy's chest, and fell back to sleep.

Chapter 22

Finn wondered if he and Troy were maybe the least cool people in New York, given that they were spending a Saturday afternoon in the Rose Reading Room at the New York Public Library. Both had their laptops open and were seated across the table from each other. Finn was doing fruitless keyword searches in journal databases, trying to find scholarship on any of their cast of characters and not coming up with much. There was a mention of Brill in a story here or there—mostly in the context of his family, and usually he was referred to as the black sheep who lived in Brooklyn— but basically nothing about Cutler, the Brill House, or even the mysterious Beauchamp.

So didn't it just figure that Troy was the first to say, "Ah, here we go."

Finn looked up. He rolled his hand to indicate Troy should speak.

In a whisper, Troy said, "I found an article in the *Times* about Nicholas Beauchamp. Apparently he was eager to build a monument to the Union dead somewhere in the city. He won over the Brill family. Our Brill had an older brother who obtained the rank of colonel and saw action at Gettysburg, among other places. He came back from the war minus a leg."

"That's surprising. I thought most of the moneyed gentlemen of New York paid for replacements to fight for them."

"Brill had another brother who did, but this first brother, whose name was Thomas R. Brill, apparently felt strongly about the Cause. His rank was probably entirely due to his family name, though."

"Yeah, yeah."

Troy grinned. He looked back at his screen. "Anyway, Brill's mother's family owned a gargantuan estate in Upper Manhattan somewhere. This was their country home, of course. Brill's mother Almira Brill, née Cummings, inherited the estate from her older brother after he died of some disease. It came into the general holdings of the Brill family in the late 1860s, but no one had time to do anything with it, and it was too far uptown to get to conveniently, so it fell into disrepair."

"How little times have changed. I always thought Upper Manhattan was dreadfully inconvenient to get to."

"Says the Columbia grad. Didn't you rent an apartment in Inwood for a while?"

"I sure did. That only made it less convenient. I could never get anyone to come home with me. I'd hit on some guy in a bar, and we'd be really into each other, and I'd invite him back to my place, then he'd go, 'You live where?' and that would be the end of that. I had a cab driver tell me once that my neighborhood didn't exist."

Troy chuckled. "Anyway. After the Panic of 1873, the Brills were looking to unload the property, if only so they wouldn't have to pay the minimal upkeep anymore. Papa Brill was always looking for ways to make charitable contributions in a way that would benefit the family in the long run. Thus the Brills were considering razing the house on the estate and donating the whole plot of land to the city to use as a park and possible site for this memorial Beauchamp was trying to make."

"You got all that from an article in the *Times*?"

"Oh, I've been researching the Brills, so I knew about

the estate already. The *Times* article talks about how Mrs. Brill wanted to use her property as a memorial site. The meat of the article, actually, is the dispute between Beauchamp and the Brills. Beauchamp was pretty firmly against Upper Manhattan as a possible site because he assumed, and was probably correct, that no one would ever see the thing if it were that far uptown."

"Exhibit A being Grant's Tomb."

"Precisely," said Troy. "City planners weren't that excited about making space for a memorial in the crowded city below Fourteenth Street, so Beauchamp was campaigning to have it built somewhere in Brooklyn. He would go on to have a hand in the creation of the Soldiers' and Sailors' Arch at Grand Army Plaza, but that wasn't until the late 1880s. Before that, he tussled with Almira Brill about locations."

"That's nice," said Finn, "but it doesn't really tell us anything besides that Beauchamp knew Brill's family. If they were planning this memorial in the mid-1870s, Theodore Brill had already been exiled to Brooklyn."

"This is totally conjecture, but what if Beauchamp decided to appeal to the Brooklyn-residing branch of the Brill family?"

Finn shook his head. "You're right, that is totally conjecture."

Troy let out a sigh. "I'm trying to connect the dots here, Finn. There's not a lot to go on."

"Don't you think we're going about this backward? We're trying to pin a murder on a guy whose name we only know because we sought shelter in his mausoleum during a rainstorm." Finn didn't disagree that looking into Beauchamp was a good idea, but he didn't like that Troy was putting all their eggs in one basket. It sure was a hell of a coincidence. The existence of ghosts was something he was willing to concede, but the idea that they'd somehow been steered to this one mausoleum when they'd gotten lost in a cemetery was too much for Finn to wrap his head around.

"Do you have an alternate suggestion?" When Finn hesitated, Troy added, "Besides, he's not just some guy. He lived in Brill's neighborhood, was about Brill's age, and had dealings with his family."

Finn rubbed his forehead. "Even so, it's a big leap from 'they knew each other' to 'he killed Brill and Cutler.'"

"So we keep digging."

Finn and Troy just looked at each other for a long time. Finn knew deep down that Troy was probably on the right track, but even if he wasn't, there wasn't much harm in pursuing it.

Troy said, "The police report indicates there was basically no sign of a struggle, right? So whoever killed Brill and Cutler was someone they knew and trusted. I doubt either man is going to be all, 'Such and So is trying to kill us!' in the journals."

"That's probably true," said Finn, "which brings me back to the old argument. What if we can't figure out who killed them?"

"We have to."

"But what if we can't? We have so little to go on. This might be one of those mysteries that's just not solvable."

"No. I refuse to believe that. Besides, at this point, we're too invested. I think that if you and I are ever going to have a future together, we have to find a way to help the ghosts. I'm convinced that if we solve this, they will be able to move on to the next plane."

After the ghosts had put him in the hospital, Finn had been thinking it might be time to give up on the case. He should have been able to just walk away. Of course, then Troy had called and cajoled him into spending his day off in the fucking library, and he'd wanted to see Troy. Maybe that made the argument that the ghosts were manipulating his feelings for Troy all the more convincing. It didn't make sense, but neither did all the emotion Finn felt where Troy was concerned.

Of course, Troy would say that Finn's involvement was necessary because some kind of magical fate thing had decreed that Finn was key to solving the case.

But probably all of this was nonsense. Probably.

Finn turned back to his computer. In the search engine, he impulsively typed in, "nicholas beauchamp homosexual."

And, bam! There was an article displayed front and center on nineteenth-century homophobia, and wouldn't you know it, Nicholas Beauchamp had led the charge.

"Well, fuck," said Finn.

"Not now, darling." Troy was looking at his own computer, but Finn could see him smiling over the top of the screen.

Finn scanned the article. "Based on this article I just found, it seems Mr. Beauchamp was quite the crusader against the demon sodomy."

Finn half expected Troy to make a joke, but instead his eyes widened. "Really?"

"Small scale, but the author dug up some pamphlet Beauchamp wrote on the evils of some of the activities going on down on the Bowery. He claims to have inadvertently wound up at some…" Finn scanned the article for the direct quotation. "Uh, 'resort for inverts' where men dressed as women and all sorts of other shenanigans."

"Perish the thought."

"He was so thoroughly disgusted that he felt it was his duty to prevent men from indulging in the sinful act of sodomy with other men."

Troy shifted in his chair and sat up straighter. He leaned across the table. "What do you think about that?"

"Well, I'm guessing his little trip through hell was not so much inadvertent as Beauchamp looking for trouble. Whether he himself was contemplating engaging in the act or if he was just looking for an excuse to get outraged, I guess we'll never know, but this is awfully peculiar, don't you think?"

"Mmm, I agree. Let me see the article."

Finn moved his laptop over to Troy, who took a few minutes to read. He looked up and said, "Here, Beauchamp comes across as, I don't know, every politician who ever stumbled into a gay scandal. 'Oh, I had no idea he was a rent boy!' Except, 'I had no idea that shady bar on the Bowery sandwiched between two brothels could possibly have any weird or illegal activities. It all seemed so wholesome!'"

"Let's skip over the part where you rub it in about being right."

Troy tapped his chin. "So what I hear you saying is that you agree that Beauchamp was a nasty piece of work who probably befriended Brill over this Civil War monument thing but then found out that Brill was actually a flaming homosexual and then killed both Brill and his lover in an angry fit one night."

"I'm saying it's a possibility I promise to try to be less

dismissive of."

"That's good enough for me." Troy smiled. "Come on, pack up. Let's celebrate your slightly more open mind by getting drunk and making out in a bar."

"Yeah, okay."

"I appreciate your enthusiasm." Troy shut down his computer and leaned closer to Finn. "If you play your cards right, maybe we'll try out some of that demon sodomy later."

* * *

They walked across town to a Hell's Kitchen bar Troy had been to a few times. It was fairly nondescript but still definitely a gay bar, what with the shirtless pretty-boy bartender and plenty of happy-hour cruising. Finn and Troy got beers and settled into a corner booth.

"I want to institute a rule," Finn said. "For the rest of the night, we do not talk about the project. No ghosts, no Victorian history, just you and me."

"Deal," said Troy, happy enough to escape for a little while.

They drank their beers and talked about television for a while. Troy tried and failed to describe the plot of a movie he'd seen recently. Finn said that he hadn't been to a movie in eons. "Loretta has me working so many hours."

"Is she making much progress with the book?"

"Yeah, some. And I think it's pretty good. Of course, I think that because I have been ghost writing parts of it."

Troy raised an eyebrow. "Really?"

"I've been trying to employ Loretta's bombastic style so it sounds like her, but yeah. She's been letting me write little passages and things when I find information I think is particularly interesting."

"It's a shame you have to mimic her. I always thought you were a good writer."

Finn's brow furrowed. "What of my writing have you even read?"

Troy shrugged. "I read a couple of the papers you wrote for Feehan when you were doing your PhD coursework."

Finn rolled his eyes. "Okay. Let's not talk about that."

"Good idea."

"How are things going with your job?" Finn sipped his beer and looked more relaxed than Troy had seen him in a while.

"Things are going well," said Troy. "I mean, relatively. I'm trying to get the KCHS to let me host more special events at the Brill House, because we're still not getting a lot of traffic. There's been a trickle, mostly local history buffs. There's a really nice garden out back that I think would be a good event space eventually, or even just a space for visitors to go, but it was pretty overgrown when the house came into our possession, and they're still cleaning it up, so it's not quite ready for people."

"You like the job?"

"I love it. This is exactly what I've always wanted to do. I mean, I wish I were curating a collection that more people cared about, but I enjoy the work a lot. And I'm writing a book."

"On Brill."

"Yeah. It started out as a biography. I was just going to put a booklet together for people who came to the Brill House. But I'm finding that I'm more interested in writing about the murder mystery, and I have more to say than can be held in a short booklet. I wrote a proposal and have been sending it around to people I know at various publishing houses and have gotten a few nibbles. Nothing for sure yet, but I don't know that I've completely settled on the right angle for it."

"Okay."

Troy shrugged. "I work six days a week most of the time. It gives me something to do during the lulls when not much is going on."

Finn nodded. He looked around the bar, his focus on Troy seeming to wane. Troy followed his gaze and found that it rested on a guy flirting with the bartender. An attractive guy flirting with the bartender. Feeling the need to win Finn's attention back, he said, "Hey."

Finn turned. "What?"

Troy kissed him. He felt Finn's body respond and knew he had Finn's attention again. He eased away but kept his hands on Finn.

Finn smirked. "I so was not checking out the guy at the bar."

Troy kissed his cheek. "Uh-huh." Then he smiled. "Maybe I just wanted to kiss you."

"Maybe you were jealous." Finn leaned in and kissed him.

It was such a pleasure to kiss him, to feel their lips slide together, to search each other for connection, to find it, to get lost in the simple sensation of the kiss.

Finn eased away. "You know, it's almost easier to talk about the ghosts."

"What?"

"I keep racking my brain for things to talk to you

about, and I keep hitting on things that are kind of negative. For example, I might have to get a new apartment because Janice is talking about moving in with her boyfriend, and I can't afford our place on my own."

"You could get another roommate."

"Don't you think it's kind of lame for a guy in his thirties to have roommates still?"

"No. I think that's how things go in New York. My assistant Genevieve has a roommate, and she's in her sixties."

"I love Janice. She's a great roommate. We get along well, we have similar feelings on how clean the apartment should be. You know? I don't want to have to adjust to living with another person."

Troy considered suggesting Finn move in with him, but he could predict how badly that conversation would go. If Finn bristled at the label "boyfriends," he'd probably go apoplectic at the thought of them shacking up.

"That's tough," he said instead. "Maybe you could get a studio or something. Or, better yet, move out of Manhattan."

"Yeah, I'll figure something out. Loretta promised me a bonus when the book gets published, so I guess I have that to look forward to. Maybe I can put that money toward a new place."

"Sure. I got my place through a broker. He charges a fee, but it's not too hefty. I'll give you his name if you want it."

Finn nodded. "Janice moving out is not a sure thing, but if she does, I'll let you know."

It was such a practical conversation. Troy smiled at Finn, and his heart did a little flip-flop when Finn chuckled and smiled back. He leaned forward and kissed Finn gently, and Finn's lips tasted of beer and that now familiar flavor that was all Finn. Finn hooked a hand behind Troy's hair and yanked a little at the strands as they kissed. Troy felt a wave of anxiety that, if they were ever able to exorcise the ghosts, Finn would just decide he couldn't let himself love Troy anymore, in which case all this would end. It was frustrating that Finn was still stubbornly hanging on to the idea that he didn't really feel what he felt, but Troy supposed that couldn't be helped. And despite Finn's reticence, Troy knew Finn felt just as strongly for him as he felt about Finn.

Finn eased away and looked at him. "You kinda spaced out on me there, Troy."

"Sorry. My mind started wandering."

"Is kissing me really so boring?"

"No. Quite the opposite. I was just thinking about how sad I would be if you ever decided I couldn't kiss you anymore."

"Or you might stop wanting to kiss me."

"I suppose. I doubt it, though."

Finn bit his lip. "You know that I…I mean, I feel like—"

"It's okay. You don't have to tell me. I understand."

"No, I do, I…" Finn looked away. "You know this is hard for me."

"I know. You asked me to table further discussion until we deal with the ghosts. I'm just happy to be spending time with you now."

"Right now? I…I love you."

Warmth spread through Troy's chest. Finn's words were nice to hear. He smiled. "Yeah, I know." He leaned over and kissed Finn again. He was surprised by how small a thing, this simple confession, could make his heart soar. He pulled Finn into a tight hug. "I love you too."

Finn kissed Troy's cheek and pulled away. His mouth was strained, like he was working hard to suppress a smile. "You want to get out of here?"

"Some Saturday night." Troy laughed. "How lame are we?"

"I don't know. It seems to be looking up."

Chapter 23

Troy spent most of the next night finishing the last volume of Brill's diary. He had to know if there were any clues.

There were. Brill wrote in January of 1878, "*Had lunch again with Mr. Beauchamp. He seems determined to pursue some sort of joint venture to build a memorial in Brooklyn to our brothers who died in the war. This is a noble cause, I told him. I said, even, that my own dear friend Mr. Cutler was a veteran. This seemed to interest Beauchamp so now I am to arrange a meeting. I mentioned this to Wash this evening, and he seemed distraught by the idea of it. 'The war is over,' he said. 'I would prefer not to remember it.'*"

He wrote in March of 1878, "*Mr. Beauchamp is a persistent fellow. I have tried telling him that I do not have the same resources that my parents do, and though I am sympathetic to his cause, I cannot help him financially. He is not hearing it. Tonight, Wash and I had him to dinner. Mrs. Morrison laid out quite a nice meal for us all. Beauchamp seemed quite taken with my Wash at first, which is natural. I suppose the fact that Wash had also been in the war gave them something in common. I thought the dinner went quite nicely, but afterward, Wash told me Mr. Beauchamp made him uncomfortable. It was not any particular words or actions, but just a feeling Wash had. I trust his instincts, but although I am not so enamored with Beauchamp, I don't see that he presents any real harm.*"

And, finally, in June of 1878, "*Mr. Beauchamp came by this evening. I did not want to invite him in because Wash and I had planned to have an intimate dinner together before retiring, but it seemed ill-mannered to turn him away. He came in and explained that he has a new venture. He has been working with Anthony Comstock to change the quality of materials being printed. Or, more specifically, he is trying to make illegal the reproduction of anything he deems lewd. Thinking it might be an interesting conversation—as I have had with individuals before, Mrs. Woodhull for example—I asked him what he considered lewd. It was as one might expect: any sort of nudity, anything that mentioned relations between men and women. Wash came into the room just at that moment and had the oddest expression on his face. I clarified that Beauchamp was listing undesirable material, which got Wash to smile. Then, thinking we were in his confidence and completely agreed with him, Beauchamp mentioned also that he'd been doing work at some establishments on the Bowery, trying to close the sorts of clubs that allowed inverted men to populate. Wash must have been feeling argumentative, because he asked Beauchamp to clarify what he meant. This led to a rather lengthy discussion of everything Beauchamp finds wrong and disgusting about sexual relations between men. I will admit that it was hard to keep my face blank."*

After he read that last part, Troy rolled over and looked at his alarm clock. It was just after 3:00 a.m. Too late to call Finn. Or was it? If Finn didn't want to talk, Troy reasoned, he could just not answer.

A very groggy-sounding Finn did pick up the phone. "This better be an emergency, asshole."

"It's Beauchamp," Troy said. "It has to be."

Finn groaned. "Can this wait until tomorrow?"

"Has Cutler mentioned Beauchamp at all?"

There was a long pause during which Troy heard some rustling. "Just that he didn't like him. I don't know. I've still got about forty pages left to read."

"Can I see you tomorrow?"

"Tomorrow's Monday. I was going to see you anyway."

"Oh, right."

"Troy, go to sleep. I can't even think right now." Finn hung up.

Troy lay back down but then read the rest of the journal. The last entry was dated August 9, 1878—ten days before Brill and Cutler were murdered—and was not particularly enlightening, though Troy found it very sweet.

"It has been exceedingly hot. Wash disobeyed Mrs. Morrison's orders and sneaked into the kitchen to make some cold tea for me. The tea was a little bitter, but it was cold, and it came from Wash. I told him I appreciated the gesture, and that I loved him despite bitter tea. I have been reluctant to write about how things really are with us, but I think by now, should anyone but myself ever read this, it will be clear that my love for him goes very deep. It is a continuing source of frustration that we must keep it a complete secret."

How complete a secret? The other men in the building knew and the diarist neighbor, Thomas Fledgling Longwood, had written about it.

He fell asleep that night contemplating that. Then he slipped into a nightmare. In the dream, a bearded man whom Troy didn't recognize barged into his apartment. He threatened both Troy and Finn, but it was Finn who bore the brunt. Finn didn't take any shit from this guy, and he argued back even when it started to seem foolish to do so. Then the bearded man punched him. Finn lashed out in return, but he was no match for this man, who had forty pounds on Finn easily. The man proceeded to beat the ever-loving shit out of Finn, throwing punches and kicking him when he fell to the ground. Finn bled and screamed in pain, but Troy's feet were bolted to the floor, and he couldn't move to help. He had to just stand there, unable to do anything, and he felt Finn's pain as his own.

The dream was devastating. He woke up wanting more than ever to call Finn and considered calling a cab and going to Finn's place just to hold him and verify that he was still okay, but by then it was five a.m., and Finn was probably still asleep and still upset that Troy had woken him earlier.

Awake and unwilling to go back to sleep, Troy got up and grabbed his computer. He spent the next two hours searching for everything there was on the Internet about Beauchamp. It wasn't a lot, but what little he did find had him convinced that Beauchamp was the murderer.

* * *

When Finn reported for duty at the Brill House that night, he was greeted by Troy, who immediately pulled Finn into his arms in a tight hug.

"Um, what?" Finn said, putting his arms around Troy.

"Sorry, just humor me. I had a really awful dream last night in which bad things happened to you, so I'm glad you're here and unharmed."

"Okay." It was hard to deny that it felt good to get squeezed tightly by Troy. Finn closed his eyes and leaned into Troy's warm body.

"Have you learned anything new?" Troy asked as he pulled away.

"I'm almost done with Cutler's journal. I read part of it on my lunch break today. I have maybe ten or fifteen pages left."

Troy nodded. Then he bent his head and kissed Finn's forehead. "I'm hungry. I'll run out and get food if you want to sit in the office and finish reading. How do you feel about Indian? I have a tikka masala craving."

"Sure."

They ordered, and Troy went off to pick up their food while Finn sat in the office finishing the journal. The last months of Cutler's life seemed to be largely filled with minutiae. He'd been helping Sam Redding study enough of the great books to get into some kind of school program. Cutler had been a big reader most of his life, despite his working-class background. He wrote a lot about the garden he was tending and kept meticulous records of how many bulbs he planted and which dates the annuals and perennials started to bloom. Sometimes he jotted down recipes. There were a few cute references to things Brill had done. "*Today Teddy brought me breakfast in bed, and it was quite delicious,*" or "*We walked to the water and gazed at the boats and talked about nothing in particular. I could not have imagined a better afternoon.*"

Then, about a week before his death, Cutler wrote his final entry. "*Teddy and I dined with Sam this evening. I believe that boy is off to a good start. I will admit I did not always like him, but Teddy was so fond of him that I could not deny him when he insisted the boy come live at the Brill House. Sam has grown on me. It turns out there are brains under that rough-and-tumble exterior. Beyond that, Mr. Beauchamp dropped by earlier today, and he was completely out of sorts about something. Teddy was out attending to some business matters, so Beauchamp had only me to speak with, which he seemed to find unsatisfactory. I inquired about the Civil War Memorial, but this was apparently a sore subject. He instead seemed to want to speak with me about his project with Mr. Comstock, but I told him I was not particularly interested in the details of that, especially since I find most censorship distasteful. Beauchamp was quite incensed. He stormed out before Teddy arrived back at home.*"

Finn thought the end unsatisfying but spared a thought for Cutler, who must have realized something was amiss before he hid his diary. Finn wondered whether Cutler knew he was in danger, or whether he hid the diary as a safety measure lest Beauchamp or someone else found it.

Finn finished with the entry right when Troy came back in with dinner. Over their meals, they exchanged details from the journal entries they'd read.

Finn shoved half a samosa in his mouth. He loved the spices used in Indian food, so he took a moment to savor them before he swallowed and said, "I agree with you that Beauchamp is the most likely suspect. Cutler clearly doesn't like him and in fact seems to delight in poking at him. I don't see how that's motivation enough for murder, though."

"I know. Something must have happened."

"We may never know what."

Troy ate a piece of chicken dripping with bright orange sauce and said, "I have an idea."

"Of course you do." Finn predicted Troy would say something outlandish. He wasn't disappointed.

"What if we went upstairs and returned to the scene of the crime, armed with the knowledge we have now. Maybe the ghosts will react."

"Alternately, we could take a look at the police report again and see if it contains anything that might be useful. Maybe there was a clue we overlooked the first time we saw the report because we didn't know about Beauchamp."

"You're so practical." There was a note of sarcasm in Troy's voice.

"Fuck you. Get out the report."

Troy riffled through a folder of case-related materials on his desk. He produced the police report and handed it to Finn. "Here, you scan this. I will tell you everything I found on the Internet about Beauchamp."

Finn looked at the report. He was particularly interested to see if the police had taken anything from the scene that might have pointed to a killer. He gave Troy enough of his attention that he heard what Troy said next.

"Beauchamp seems to have had two claims to fame." Troy leaned forward, resting his elbows on the desk. "First, he had a hand in the creation of Grand Army Plaza. He worked hard to get a Civil War memorial in Brooklyn. There's also some statuary around Borough Hall that was his doing. He was especially fond of Henry Ward Beecher, actually. He wrote a few essays praising the preacher."

"Huh. That's interesting."

"Especially given his other claim to fame. Beauchamp teamed up with Anthony Comstock to work on anti-obscenity legislation. Comstock ultimately concentrated on lewd materials being sent through the mail, an achievable goal, but Beauchamp wanted to go a step further and was trying to close down brothels in Brooklyn. There was one especially notorious one in what is now Park Slope that was a particular bugaboo for Beauchamp."

Finn chuckled. "I doubt he had a lot of luck with that."

"He didn't. For every brothel he managed to get shut down, three more sprang up. The thing with this brothel in Park Slope that is especially curious is that, in addition to being a place for men to find a certain breed of lady, there were a number of men on staff. It was a place in which it was generally accepted that all men had needs that needed to be met, and so they would accommodate everyone. Cock or pussy, take your pick."

"Did Beauchamp object to the brothel generally or the male prostitutes specifically?"

"It's not clear from what I read, but I have a guess."

Finn did too. "Okay."

"Here's my favorite part. Beauchamp attended services at the Plymouth Church of the Pilgrims every Sunday. As I'm sure you know, that was Henry Ward Beecher's pulpit.

Comstock had a lot of nasty things to say about the Beecher adultery scandal, but the most scathing comments he had were for guess who?"

Finn knew. He put his food aside and sat up. "Victoria Woodhull and her sister Tennessee Claflin. They were right at the center of Comstock's campaign. I can't believe I forgot that."

"Right. Apparently Beauchamp was right there with Comstock, condemning the sisters."

"If I remember correctly, Comstock hated them primarily because they published some racy material in their newspaper." Finn mentally ran through everything he knew about Comstock. "He had the sisters and Woodhull's second husband, Colonel Blood, arrested and thrown in jail for printing obscene materials."

"Right. The impetus for that was Woodhull's decision to print the details of the Beecher adultery scandal."

Finn shook his head. "I can't believe how circular all this is. Beauchamp was involved with Comstock, who got Victoria Woodhull thrown in jail for printing obscene material related to Henry Ward Beecher, whom Beauchamp apparently would have defended to the death."

"Precisely." Troy grinned.

"But, of course, Beauchamp was more scandalized by the printing of the details in the paper and not by Beecher's adulterous behavior itself, which doesn't matter that much because Beauchamp seemed to be particularly crusading against homosexual lewd conduct, yes?"

"Yup. My guess is that he got into some kind of argument with Brill or Cutler or both of them."

"Probably Cutler. He seems the more ornery of the

two."

"Yes. Beauchamp spent a lot of time courting Brill in the financial sense because he wanted the Brill family to invest in his memorial. But then he learned that a man he thought was his ally was actually one of the inverts he loudly condemned, and he was so angry and horrified that he killed the lovers."

Finn agreed this was likely the scenario. "One catch. How did he get to the bedroom? Cutler didn't trust Beauchamp. It seems unlikely they would have just invited him upstairs."

"Yeah, that part's still kind of a mystery."

Finn went back to looking at the police report. It was frustratingly lacking in details. No sign of a struggle, nothing peculiar found at the crime scene. There was a lengthy and full catalog of what had been found in the bedroom, but most of it seemed like it should have been there. The only odd thing was a stray cuff link.

"The police found an onyx cuff link, but it could have been anybody's." Finn frowned. "Forensic science was so far behind what it is now. I think today, cops would work overtime to figure out who owned that cuff link. If it was Beauchamp's, it would have put Beauchamp in the bedroom, and that's an awfully suspicious place for him to be. But one onyx cuff link that might have belonged to any of these men doesn't tell us anything, especially when these detectives didn't bother to follow up." Frustrated, Finn rolled up the report and hit it against the desk.

Troy packed up his food. He slid one plastic container into the minifridge in the corner.

"I feel like we're still missing something," said Finn.

"I agree, but I'm out of places to look."

Finn thought about it. Going upstairs seemed like a completely ridiculous thing to do. What would staring at Brill and Cutler's old bedroom really do? Would looking at the crime scene jog memories they didn't have? And what was special about tonight? How was it different than any of a dozen other nights that they'd stood in that bedroom? Yet Finn felt an irrational desire to go there. Was it his own thinking that led him to that desire, or was he being manipulated again?

He looked up and saw Troy analyzing him.

Troy said, "You want to go upstairs."

"More than anything."

They packed up the rest of the food and walked to the staircase.

When they first stepped into the bedroom, nothing happened. Finn and Troy stood at the foot of the bed, contemplating it. Then Troy said, "Hold my hand."

"What?"

"It's just a hunch I have. Like we'd be combining our powers. Hold my hand."

Finn was skeptical about that accomplishing anything, but he did as he was told, sliding his hand into Troy's, intertwining their fingers.

Then Finn was transported. That was the only way he could explain it. His feet never left the floor, but suddenly he was back in the lobby, only it wasn't the lobby as he knew it. There was more stuff in it, the floor tiling was different, and a couch sat where the information desk should have been. There was a staircase in place of the elevator. Finn, as Wash Cutler, stood back as Teddy let in a short, bearded man with dark blond hair. Finn knew this was Nicholas Beauchamp.

Teddy was saying, "We were not expecting you, Mr. Beauchamp. How delightful." There was no enthusiasm in his voice.

"I only have a few minutes, but I have a few things I very much wish to discuss with you."

Teddy nodded. "All right. Mr. Cutler, would you inform Mrs. Morrison that we'd like to have tea in the parlor?"

"Yes, of course," said Finn, and he could feel Wash's deep hatred for Beauchamp. He walked to the kitchen—which was on the first floor, where a small gallery was located in Finn's time—and found it empty. He remembered that it was Mrs. Morrison's day off. He put water on the stove to boil but then realized the stove had gone cool and would take a while to warm up again. With a sigh, he gave up on the tea but decided his guest was undeserving anyway.

Finn went back to the lobby and climbed the stairs where the elevator should have been. He found Teddy and Beauchamp sitting across from each other in the parlor, with Beauchamp taking up a lot of space on the sofa and Teddy sitting on the edge of the chaise.

"We forgot it is Mrs. Morrison's day off. I could make tea, but it will take a little while," Finn said.

When Finn looked at Teddy, he imagined he could see Troy inside. Their eyes met, and an understanding of sorts passed between them. At minimum, he knew Troy was there with him, and he found that comforting.

Teddy, however, looked upset. He was frowning and had his arms crossed over his chest. "That's all right. I don't think Mr. Beauchamp will be staying very long, after all."

Finn felt some happiness in that fact, but said, "Oh? Why is that?"

"I am merely stating facts, Brill," said Beauchamp.

"I will not be insulted in my own home."

Beauchamp spared Finn a look that was full of hostility. His sneer was malicious enough to make Finn take a step back. To Teddy, Beauchamp said, "I did not insult you."

Teddy stood. "No, you implied something about Mr. Cutler that might as well have been an insult. As Mr. Cutler is my dear friend, I take any insult paid to him as if it were paid to me."

Finn/Wash was curious about what Beauchamp had said, but also sensed this was going to go badly. "I'm sure it is nothing. Sit back down, Teddy."

Teddy remained standing and looked intently at Finn/Wash as if he were trying to communicate something psychically. Finn knew intellectually what was going to happen, and his fear mounted. Bile rose up his esophagus. He worked hard to keep his face calm, though he realized that he was a passive observer here. Beauchamp wouldn't be able to see any of Finn's turmoil on his face. He'd only be able to see Wash, and Wash still didn't know what was coming.

Beauchamp stood also. "You have a ward, Mr. Brill, a young man named Sam, do you not?"

"I do. That is, he is a teenage boy that I look after sometimes. He has a room here, though he does not sleep here every night."

"Is he here now?"

"No. He went out a little while ago."

Finn realized that no one was home. No Mrs. Morrison, no Sam, and, it seemed, no tenants upstairs. No one to overhear an argument. Or a gunshot.

Beauchamp began pacing. "I spoke with young Master Redding briefly the last time he was here. He's an intelligent young man."

"Yes, I think so," said Teddy. There was a question in his voice. Finn imagined he was trying to ascertain where Beauchamp was going with this line of inquiry.

"He certainly likes you a great deal."

Wash caught on before Teddy did. "I do not like the implication you are making, Mr. Beauchamp," he said.

Beauchamp raised an eyebrow. "What implication? I merely stated that the boy seems to like Mr. Brill."

"If you are thinking that Teddy's affections for the boy are anything but fatherly, then you are mistaken."

Beauchamp took a step toward Wash. "Are you jealous?"

"Of course not. I know the truth of the situation, is all."

"The Greeks had a tradition of men bedding boys, did they not? Filthy practice. It is a good thing that Christianity came through to civilize them. But I understand some men still adhere to the Greek ways."

"Not Teddy."

Beauchamp's gaze traveled from Wash's head to his toes. Finn hated that gaze, could feel the malice in it. "No," Beauchamp said. "Teddy does not lie with *boys*, does he? He lies with you."

Teddy bristled. "You will leave now, Mr. Beauchamp."

"Master Redding mentioned that Mr. Cutler also lived on this floor, but I see only one other room."

"I will escort you out," Teddy said, moving toward the

door.

But Beauchamp wasn't budging now. "You are both disgusting. An abomination in the eyes of God."

"I don't have to listen to this," Wash/Finn said. He intended to storm out of the room, but as he turned to go, Beauchamp pulled a gun.

It did not escape Finn's attention that it was a derringer. Specifically, it was a two-shot, silver-plated derringer that caught the light from the chandelier in the parlor. It was almost beautiful. Finn might have thought so if he could forget how deadly the weapon was.

He had an alarming thought. If he were inhabiting Wash's body, would he feel the shot too? Would some harm come to him?

More to the point, could he change events? Could he save Wash and Teddy?

He looked at Teddy. Panic was etched all over his face. Finn's heart raced, and his stomach tightened; he could not remember ever feeling so terrified. He was about to get shot. He knew he was. It was inevitable. He could no more change how this was about to go down than he could change history. The longer the showdown dragged out, the more trouble he had breathing, the more nauseated he became. Beads of sweat broke out all over his body. Beauchamp was going to shoot him. He was certain.

Beauchamp motioned for Teddy and Wash to go back out into the hallway. "You may know," he said, "I have made it my mission to eradicate the unholy from the city, and you certainly stand as shining beacons of unholy."

"How long have you known?" Finn heard himself ask.

Beauchamp looked at Wash curiously. "You are a clever

one, Mr. Cutler. I have known since last week. Something young Sam said in conversation aroused my suspicion that the two of you were entangled in some sort of sexual liaison. Seeing you now just confirms it for me."

Beauchamp advanced, and by instinct, Finn backed up. Teddy did the same. They stepped back, their arms up. Finn tripped backward into the bedroom and steadied himself by grabbing the door frame.

"You intended to kill us when you came here tonight," Teddy said. He took a step back to stand with Finn/Wash.

"No," said Beauchamp. "I wanted confirmation of my suspicions, but I did not have a particular plan to kill you until they now."

Teddy gave Wash/Finn a petrified look, his eyes wide, his mouth agape. Then he turned back to Beauchamp. "Spare us!" he said.

"I will not," Beauchamp said.

He fired.

The bullet hit Teddy square in the chest, and he collapsed on the floor. Wash let out a cry of anguish and knelt next to him. He put his hand over the wound and felt the futility in the action. Blood oozed out and then gushed through Wash's fingers. But Teddy moved. "Wash," he said.

"I'm here."

Teddy bit his lip and nodded. He whispered. "Remember above all things that I love you."

"Please, stay with me."

But Teddy stopped talking. He stared at something behind Wash. Finn heard Beauchamp advancing and knew what was to come.

"I love you, as well, more than I love this life," Finn

said.

Then there was a crash, and everything went black.

* * *

Death had come slowly for Theodore Cummings Brill. The bullet had not done enough damage to kill him instantly. Instead, he'd lain bleeding on the floor, the life oozing out of him with each pump of his heart. He needed to scream, but he was unable to speak or call out. He was alive long enough to see Beauchamp shoot Wash in the head. That had hurt more than the bullet wound to his own chest. Wash—and Finn within him, Troy had thought as he watched the scene play out—was dead before he hit the floor; Teddy watched the life vanish from his body almost instantly. Beauchamp had taken the time to pose Wash with the gun in his hand before he ran from the room. The front door slammed.

As he lay there staring at Wash's lifeless face, it occurred to Troy that if this shooting had happened in his time, Beauchamp's fingerprints would have been found all over the gun. Instead, the murder remained a cold case for more than a century.

He had a lot of time to think as he lay dying.

Troy thought of the pain he felt, as real as if he'd been shot in the chest himself, blinding, excruciating, throbbing whenever he inhaled. He thought about Finn and wondered if he'd felt any pain when he'd been shot—he hoped not. He thought about his life back in his own time. Would Finn stick around now that they'd solved the mystery? Would he even live himself, or had the bullet killed him as surely as it had killed Wash?

It was awful how Brill had to die, so slowly, right there on the floor next to his dead lover. There was nothing he could do. He'd wanted to kill himself, to end his own misery as fast as he could, but he was unable to move, and there was nothing within arm's reach that would have done the job. He worried for a while that he'd live, that someone would find him and save him. What use was his life if Wash was dead? With Wash gone for certain, all joy left Teddy.

Eventually, everything had turned green, then gray, then black.

* * *

Troy came to first. He sat up off the floor and rubbed his chest. The pain was receding but still very present. It was emotional as well as physical pain such as he had never felt before. Because he'd had to lie there.

He looked around the darkened bedroom exhibit. Finn lay on the floor beside him, unconscious but breathing.

Troy started to cry. He crawled over to Finn. He pulled Finn's limp body into his arms and held him tightly.

He felt awful, but at the same time, Troy was grateful that Finn was still there, still alive, that he and Finn still had a chance together. The pain in his chest had lessened, but he was still tense as he thought about what he'd witnessed. His relief and his love for Finn were so intense the emotions seemed to bubble over and out of him. He held Finn tighter, and he wept.

Finn stirred. Troy eased away and helped him sit up. Finn frowned.

When Finn faltered, Troy wrapped his arms around him again and pressed his face into his shoulder. He felt Finn's arms come around him. Finn made comforting murmurs but didn't say any real words. Troy felt him shiver but didn't think he was crying.

After a significant amount of time passed, Finn said, "That was intense."

"It was terrible. Teddy outlived Wash by almost an hour. He just lay there on the floor, unable to move, next to his dead lover."

"That's awful."

That was an understatement. Troy had never experienced anything so horrible, and he found it hard to come up with the words to describe it. Holding Finn, feeling the life pulse through his body, went a long way to ease the pain he felt.

Eventually, he pulled away from Finn and looked around. "Well," he said, addressing the ghosts more than Finn. "We know what happened now. You are free."

There was a gentle rumbling under the floor. The light in the room went blindingly bright. Two beams grew from near where Troy and Finn sat on the floor. A flash lit up the room, like an explosion. Then everything went dark again. And quiet. Eerily quiet.

Finn gasped. "They're gone."

Indeed, the absence of the ghosts was palpable. Troy felt it as a sudden emptiness. He was a little sad about their passing, but he knew it was for their own good. The mystery had been solved. Troy and Finn had finished Brill and Cutler's unfinished business. Finally, their souls were allowed to move on.

Troy stood up. Finn did too, a moment later. What Troy needed to know more than anything was whether or not Finn's feelings for him had changed now that the ghosts were gone. He couldn't bring himself to ask, though, fearing they had. Troy knew he was still very much in love with Finn. It would break his heart if he lost both the ghosts and Finn in the same night.

Finn looked pensive, his brow furrowed. He contemplated the floor where they had so recently lain. "Now what?"

"I don't know. I suppose all this will go into my book. I'll have to posit this as a theory of the crime, not the truth, since there's no way anyone would ever believe me. But at least then some semblance of justice will be done. And you and I will know the truth, if nothing else."

Finn nodded.

"Did you feel anything? When Beauchamp shot you?"

"No. I heard a noise, and then everything went dark."

Troy thanked whatever deity there was for small favors. "That's good. That means Wash never felt any pain."

A look of horror came over Finn's face. "You felt it?"

Troy nodded.

"Are you all right?"

Troy rubbed his chest. The pain was gone now. "I feel okay. I might be in shock. We'll see how I feel tomorrow, I suppose." He tried to smile.

Finn glanced back toward the doorway. "I think I need to go home."

Troy's heart sank. He felt sick as the horrible disappointment sank in. He supposed this was really it. He still loved Finn, but Finn, perhaps, did not return the sentiment. Troy figured it was better not to dwell on it. "Yes, all right."

"You too, Troy. You look a little traumatized."

Troy nodded.

Finn took a deep breath. "I feel like I should say

something here, but I'm speechless."

"That's all right. I don't need a speech." He put some effort into making that smile form this time. He didn't want the kiss-off, anyway. "So I guess this is good-bye for a while, huh?"

Finn looked surprised, but he nodded, and Troy felt that deep in his gut, felt the finality of the moment, the end of their time together. He missed Finn already, and Finn hadn't even left.

"I'm sure I'll see you around," Finn said. "We can't seem to keep from running into each other."

Troy nodded and walked toward the bedroom door. "So that's it? The project ends and so do we?"

Finn shrugged. "We knew this was the likely outcome."

"Seriously? All these weeks we've spent together? None of that meant anything?"

"What do you want me to say?" Finn walked toward the staircase. "I guess we…" Then he stopped and shook his head. "I need to go. I'll see you around, Troy." He walked out of the room before Troy could speak.

Chapter 24

Finn stormed into the Brill House the next morning, feeling like he was being followed by a rain cloud. Genevieve sat at the information desk, reading a paperback romance novel. "Hey, Finn," she said cheerily when he approached the desk.

"Hi, is Troy here? I need to talk to him."

Genevieve glanced toward Troy's office. The door was closed. "He's here, but he's not seeing anybody."

"He'll see me."

"He told me not to let anyone into his office."

"He will see me." Without waiting for a response, Finn marched over to the office door and opened it.

Troy was at his desk, sitting with his face in his hands. Finn closed the door again.

"Troy? Are you okay?"

"Finn?" He looked up and frantically wiped at his eyes.

Finn flashed on the scene of Troy weeping the night before. He'd never seen Troy cry. He'd spent all night thinking about that. What had made Troy weep like that? Was it because he was in pain from the shooting? Had he felt the same anguish Finn had at the end?

"What are you doing here?" Troy asked.

"I had to see you. Are you crying?"

"No." He was very clearly crying. "I wonder if this is what women feel like after they have babies. It's like post-exorcism depression."

Finn sat in the guest chair. "Yeah. I know a little about that."

Troy pulled a tissue from the box on his desk and blew his nose. After he tossed the tissue in a trash can, he said, "I feel really awful, Finn. Can you just say what you're going to say and then go so I can go back to wallowing?"

Finn wasn't sure how to voice what he wanted Troy to know. He'd spent all morning thinking about how to say it and still couldn't articulate it. He supposed that being asked to cut to the chase was probably good. It meant he could say what he needed to, bear the brunt of whatever Troy had to hurl at him, and then leave. Maybe then, hopefully, they'd be able to put it all behind them. He took a breath and said, "I woke up this morning feeling worse than I've felt in a really long time. I'd say by the look on your face that this is true for you also."

Troy nodded.

"It took me a little while to figure out why. Aside from the obvious, I mean. What we went through last night, the ghosts, the shooting, everything, that was horrible. But there was more to it than that. How I felt this morning, I mean. I'm not saying this well."

Troy took a deep breath. He smiled weakly, then looked at his desk. "You're doing okay. You said it took you a while to figure it out. What did you come up with?"

Finn's first instinct was to ask more about how Troy felt. Knowing how what he had to say would be received would make saying it easier. Of course, that was the easy way, and Finn figured doing this the hard way would go further to prove that what he had to say was true.

He took a moment to gather his thoughts. Then he said, "I felt awful because you weren't with me."

Troy looked up. "What?"

"So it turns out that, despite what I expected, I'm still

in love with you. I was stupid to just leave last night. I woke up this morning still thinking about what happened, and what I felt more than anything was that I wished you had been there with me this morning, that we could talk about what happened, or not, as long as we did whatever we did together."

Troy just sat there staring, which Finn found unnerving. "Despite what you expected?" Troy said.

"I don't know if you caught my larger point there, but that's not important. I mean, you know what I was thinking while we worked on the case. I thought we were being manipulated, and we were, but the ghosts are gone now, and my feelings haven't changed, okay? You were right all along, at least as far as I was concerned. If that's not the case for you, you should tell me soon so that I can get to Loretta's before she fires me for being so late."

Troy looked down again. Finn wasn't sure exactly what he expected, but it wasn't the somber air in the room. It wasn't Troy sitting there saying nothing. The longer Troy dragged it out, the more Finn's stomach flopped. Perhaps he hadn't imagined that Troy's feelings had changed, that he was the only one whose feelings had carried over. If that was the case, how the fuck he was going to get through life without Troy now?

Very slowly, Troy stood. Sensing he was about to get escorted out, Finn stood also. He looked down at his feet and willed himself not to let his emotions show on his face. Then, before Finn could figure out what was happening, he found himself wrapped up in Troy's arms.

"You idiot," Troy said, crying openly now. "Don't you know how I feel? I love you so much, and I thought when you left last night that you were done with me, same as the ghosts were, and it was the worst night I have ever had in my life."

Finn put his arms around Troy. "Shit," he said. "I'm so sorry for running out. I was overwhelmed by what I was feeling, and I freaked out. I should have stayed, but I panicked."

Troy let out a watery laugh. "I forgive you if you promise not to ever do that again."

Finn pressed his body into Troy's. "You keep telling me I'm an idiot. I don't know if I can promise not to do stupid things."

"Not that," Troy said. He gently kissed the side of Finn's face. "I mean, first of all, you are an idiot for thinking all that time we spent together meant nothing. Maybe the ghosts were pushing us together, but all those hours we sat in this office just talking, or in my apartment making love, or in the library or on the Promenade, that all meant something. And it turns out that you and I are really good together, ghosts or not, and no one can manipulate what we feel for each other. And, because you're a pigheaded, stubborn bastard, odds are pretty good that you will do more stupid things over the course of our relationship, and I can't make you promise not to. Just…don't ever leave me alone like that again."

"Well. That's a promise I think I can keep. Although you'll forgive me for leaving in a few minutes, since I'm already late for work, and you have an actual job to do as well."

"Just this once. But let me hold you for another minute."

Finn was fine with that. He pressed his hands into Troy's back, and they stood there together, arms around each other, in the middle of Troy's office. Finn was conscious of the minutes ticking by, of Loretta's anger mounting as he got later and later, but right then, he didn't much care. He was with Troy, and that was what mattered.

Epilogue

Finn sat in the last row of chairs in the small event room in the basement of the Brill House. He watched people trickle in, wondering what the turnout would be like. The number of people seated had already blown Finn's expectations out of the water; he'd been thinking there would be a few people from the Kings County Historical Society and probably a bunch of Troy's grad school friends. But a bunch of strangers, including a man Finn recognized as the chairman of a local gay rights group, had shown up for the event.

Darnell and Mark slipped into chairs on either side of Finn. "I see you hiding back here," said Darnell.

"I'm trying to be inconspicuous."

Darnell nodded. "We haven't seen you in a while. How's school?"

"All right. As of a week ago, I'm done with classes." Finn was a dissertation shy of finally finishing his PhD. "Troy is leaning on me to write my dissertation on George Washington Cutler."

"I think that is an excellent idea," said Darnell. "Where *is* Helen?"

Finn gestured behind him. "He claimed to be warming up, but I'm guessing he's having a nervous breakdown in the men's room."

"This *is* a big deal," said Mark.

"Have you read the book yet?" asked Darnell.

"I read the manuscript while he was writing it. He made the *Times* bestseller list, you know," said Finn, unable to keep the pride out of his voice.

"Well, *well*," said Darnell. "I don't know if I'm more impressed by the bestseller news or the fact that you're gushing so much."

"Those jokes about how Troy and I used to hate each other got old a long time ago."

"You guys sniped at each other for more than a decade," said Mark. "We've only had, what, two years to adjust to you as a couple."

"Whatever."

Mark grinned and looked at Darnell. "Honey, can I wear the blue suit to their wedding?"

"Ooh, yes. Should I wear that dark red shirt?"

"Guys!" said Finn. "Knock it off. There's no wedding."

Troy's boss stepped up to the podium at the front of the room. Finn had met the man on a number of occasions now, mostly KCHS functions. Usually just the spouses of employees attended, but somewhere around the time Troy had started referring to Finn as his "partner" instead of his "boyfriend," Finn had become a regular fixture at KCHS events.

The man at the podium spoke. "Hello, everyone. I'm Stanley Williams, the chairman of the Kings County Historical Society." There was a brief burst of polite applause. "It is my great honor to introduce to you Troy Rafferty. He is one of my favorite people, and I think we've got an exciting talk coming up tonight. Troy is the curator of this very museum, and he has written a book called *Ghosts in the Parlor: The Search for Love and Justice in a Gilded-Age Mystery*. Let's give him a round of applause."

The audience clapped. Troy trotted up to the podium

and nodded. He was wearing a dark suit; Troy looked good on most occasions, but he oozed sex in the suit he had on.

Troy scanned the crowd. His gaze met Finn's, and he nodded. "Good evening," he said to the crowd. "I thought I'd start by reading a few passages from the book, and then I'll open up the floor to questions." He cleared his throat and flipped open his copy of the book.

Finn knew he was worried either that he'd fall on his face during the talk or that someone in the audience would react negatively to some of the content in the book. Finn thought the appearance of a gay rights leader indicated that most of the audience probably knew what they were in for.

Troy started to read. *"The Brill House's first owner was a man named Theodore Cummings Brill. He was the youngest son of a prominent New York family. He moved to Brooklyn in 1871, more or less exiled there by his family. In his journals, he writes about some event that precipitated this but never describes the event. Based on how things would unfold over the next seven years, my best guess has been for some time that Brill was caught in a compromising situation with another man."* Troy then launched into the briefest of biographies, mentioning Cutler and ending with Brill's untimely death. Finn knew the book went much further in depth, but he was content to listen to Troy's voice as it rolled over him.

After he finished the passage, Troy paused. "This book has two components to it. It's both Brill's story and my own. I don't think I'm overstating the case when I say that my life changed significantly while I was searching for answers about what happened to Brill. So this part of the book is a little more personal." He flipped to a different page. He took a deep breath and cleared his throat again. *"I first met Christopher Finnegan when we were both undergraduate students at Columbia. I can't honestly say we were friends. Our relationship always felt more adversarial than that. But we did have a lot in common, more than he would probably ever admit to. We were both history majors with particular interest in the Gilded Age. We both like trivia and read serious nonfiction for fun. We both grew up in the suburbs. We were both gay.*

"*For fourteen years, Finn and I bounded in and out of each other's lives. Our paths crossed often, both academically and socially. We got drunk together a few times. We argued a lot. I vacillated between wanting to romance him and hoping never to see him again.*

"*I didn't expect anything different the day he showed up at the Brill House to take a tour. He was working with writer Loretta Kitteredge on a book about Victoria Woodhull.*" Here Troy paused and looked up. "That book came out six months ago, for the curious. Finn wrote an essay about Woodhull and the feminist movement that's included as one of the appendixes. It's really good." He swallowed and looked back at the book, then resumed reading.

"*We bickered as I led him around the museum. At some point, it dawned on me that not only would I need another pair of eyes on the project of figuring out the mystery of what happened to Theodore Cummings Brill, but that Finn, who also had a background in nineteenth-century history and Victoriana, would be the ideal person to help me. Aside from the fact that he was smart and capable, I knew he wouldn't humor or indulge me. If I went down the wrong path, he'd tell me so in no uncertain terms. Which is what happened. Often.*" He looked up and grinned, and the audience laughed.

Finn hadn't heard most of this before. He knew he was featured prominently in the book, but this bit of background hadn't been in the first draft.

Troy closed the book and looked at the audience. "One thing I can say is that this book is pretty tempered. I am not ashamed to admit that I am prone to flights of fancy sometimes, and one thing Finn excels at is telling me when I'm being ridiculous. That sounds like a criticism, but I promise I'm not being sarcastic. He's a lot more skeptical than I am generally. He doesn't believe a hypothesis until he has lots of evidence to corroborate it. I think that's why we work together so well. I'd propose something really outlandish, and he would go out of his way to prove me wrong, and then we'd arrive at the truth. I pursued avenues he wouldn't have looked at, and I like to think I opened his mind."

Troy paused and looked down. "I think it was also helpful to have someone with a certain…perspective to help with the project. Once we knew for sure that Brill and Cutler were engaged in a homosexual relationship, we spent a lot of time talking about how being gay was a different experience in Brill's day. I related to Brill in a way I hadn't expected to when I started the project. Not that our lives are parallel. Quite the contrary. And not that there's even some universal gay experience. But I felt for him when I read his journals and read about his struggles to accept himself and his situation. I think we all go through that process to a certain extent. Finn related to it too. It was nice to have a research partner who got it like Finn did."

A happy warmth spread through Finn's chest. He was genuinely touched. Troy complimented Finn all the time and was even sometimes quite effusive in his praise, but this was not something he'd ever said aloud to Finn before. Finn wanted to run up to the stage and throw his arms around Troy, but Troy still had the podium, and he was still talking.

"I don't think it spoils the book to tell you that Finn and I fell in love over the course of our investigation into Brill's death." Troy smiled. "I think sometimes about how lucky we are to be a couple now instead of in the 1870s. I mean, I'm talking about this openly with you all, for one thing. About a year and a half ago, we got an apartment together a few blocks from here, and the landlord knows we're a couple. We live in a time when it's legal for us to get married, even. I wonder sometimes what Brill and Cutler would have thought of the state of things today. They were in what was basically a committed relationship for almost five years when they were killed. Cutler writes in his journal often about feeling ashamed. Would he have felt less of that if he lived in a time when he and Brill could have lived openly? Would they have gotten married? Would they have lived happily to a ripe old age?"

Troy looked around. He swallowed. "Well, anyway. Enough about me. I'll open up the floor for questions now."

Mark leaned across Finn's lap and said to Darnell, "Seriously, the blue suit."

"Yes, sweetie," said Darnell. "And you know the tie with the little red diamonds on it? You should wear that. And speaking of color, Finn, if you decide your groomsmen should have matching vests or something, I look especially good in green."

Finn rolled his eyes. "Will you guys cut it out?"

Most of the questions for Troy related to the meat of the book. Finn couldn't tell if the audience was uncomfortable with the Big Gay Reveal, or if they were just less interested in Troy's personal life. Actually, most of the people there wanted to know about the ghosts. Troy had thought long and hard about how much of the paranormal element to include in his book and ultimately cut out a lot of what he and Finn and seen and experienced together, figuring most readers wouldn't believe it. Finn had argued it wasn't relevant anyway; the ghosts had provided them with leads, but they did most of the legwork the old-fashioned way. Still, in the book's introduction, Troy had mentioned reports through the years about weird sightings in the house, and he left the existence of ghosts an open question.

Troy assured his audience that he was convinced the Brill House was not haunted. (*Anymore*, Finn thought.) He played the part of the indulgent skeptic surprisingly well, though, letting various people put forth theories about the unexplained phenomena in the house. He concluded by saying he thought Brill and Cutler were ultimately best served by the resolution of the mystery.

Stanley Williams gave some closing remarks that Finn didn't listen to, preoccupied now with being proud of Troy for handling himself well during his first big talk about the book. Stanley invited guests to mingle, so Finn left Darnell and Mark to contemplate flower arrangements while he walked over to Troy.

"Hi," Troy said, looking a little relieved. "Did you like the reading?"

"You're a sentimental fool, you know that?"

Troy smiled. "Yes, but I'm *your* sentimental fool. What can I say? You bring it out of me."

Finn rolled his eyes and pulled Troy into a hug. "I love you," he whispered. Troy chuckled in his ear and embraced him warmly.

Troy pulled away and said, "After all these people leave, I want to talk to you about something."

And Finn just knew. He didn't get those punch-in-the-gut feelings like he had when the ghosts were around much anymore, but occasionally he and Troy seemed to share a brainwave, and he knew exactly what Troy wanted to talk about. He wondered if Darnell and Mark did too, or if they were just making coincidental conjecture. "Oh, no," he said.

"What?" said Troy.

"Nothing. Just…congratulations on your reading. I think you did very well. And some of the things you said about me were…sweet."

"Sweet?" Troy narrowed his eyes. Then he laughed. "Oh, Finn. The way to your heart is paved with heavy books and compliments on your academic prowess. I think that's one of the things I love about you the most. If I were to compliment you on the shirt you're wearing, which I like a lot, by the way, you'd tell me to fuck off, but if I tell you how brilliant that paper you wrote on Comstock was, you'd be putty in my hands."

Before Finn could react to that, Stanley appeared and greeted Finn. There was small talk about what he'd been up to. Now that his PhD coursework was done, Finn had taken a part-time job at the Museum of the City of New York while he finished his dissertation; his current project involved setting up an exhibit on vaudeville, which he was enjoying. Troy looked on, absently running his fingers along the hair at the back of Finn's neck. Troy had been right; Finn thought compliments on his appearance were fairly meaningless, but knowing Troy respected him as a scholar, considered him an equal, that meant the world to Finn.

Genevieve came over to gossip. A few audience members came up to Troy to compliment him and ask follow-up questions. He spoke to everyone with humility and good humor. One woman came up to them and said, "I just read the book over the weekend. You must be Finn! I feel like I already know you."

When she was gone, Finn said, "I'm never coming to another of your readings."

Finally, things wound down, and people started to

leave. Mark and Darnell came over to say good-bye. They each congratulated Troy, and Darnell left with a parting remark about a banquet hall he knew of in Brooklyn.

Genevieve offered to close up the building. Troy said, "Nah, I'll do it. I have to get something from my office before we can leave, anyway." He took Finn's hand and led the way.

Finn stood in the doorway of the office as Troy riffled through papers on his desk.

"So Finn. I know you are not usually one for copious outflows of emotion, so I have something I want to say, but I'll keep it short." He opened a drawer in his desk. "I don't need a lot of ceremony, right? We just do this and get our happily ever after and that's it."

"What are you talking about?"

Troy pulled something out of his desk drawer and tossed it at Finn before Finn could see what it was. He caught it and saw it was a jewelry box. He was going to kill Darnell. Although the happy pace his heart rate kicked up to was hard to ignore. He opened the box and saw it contained two thin silver rings.

"I'll do the bended-knee thing if you want," said Troy.

The practical approach was so unexpected from Troy that Finn couldn't do much more than stare at the rings for a long moment. So, of course, Troy ruined the moment by babbling.

"Ever since the book came out, I've been thinking about how we have all these opportunities that Brill and Cutler didn't, that we can be out in public, that we don't have to lie or play games. I just told a room full of people that I'm in love with you and no one even batted an eyelash. I feel like we should grab these opportunities while we can, make the most of our life together, do something that Brill and Cutler couldn't. I think that's the best way to honor them and each other."

Finn looked at Troy. "Shut up."

Troy bit his lip. "I fucked it up, didn't I? Because I've thought about this a lot. I want to spend the rest of my life with you, and I really think that—"

"You're still talking. Come here."

Troy walked out from around the desk and approached Finn slowly. When he was in grabbing range, Finn took his hand. He pulled one of the rings out of the box—the slightly smaller one, since Troy had thinner fingers, and wasn't it curious that Troy had taken the time to get them sized in advance?—and, with shaking hands, slid the ring down Troy's left ring finger.

"Oh," said Troy.

"It was perfect."

Troy nodded and took the other ring out of the box. He slowly slid it on Finn's finger, and his hands shook even more. "So that's a yes?"

"Of course I will marry you, you idiot."

Troy pulled Finn into his arms. "Mmm. I love you. I was a little worried you'd make me wait and take time to think about it."

"Darnell mentioned it as a serious possibility a while ago, and I've been thinking about it ever since. I decided for certain two weeks ago. You're just more proactive than I am."

Troy laughed. "I'm glad we're on the same page."

Finn decided the best way to seal this deal was with a kiss. Troy kissed him back enthusiastically, as always. Finn was surprised by how happy he felt. He only hoped this meant he didn't have to spend too much time with the other spouses of KCHS employees at parties. He found himself laughing.

"What's so funny?" Troy asked.

"Nothing, I'm just happy. Come on, let's go home."

About the Author

Kate McMurray is an award-winning author of gay romance and an unabashed romance fan. When she's not writing, she works as a nonfiction editor, dabbles in various crafts, and is maybe a tiny bit obsessed with baseball. She has served on the boards of the Rainbow Romance Writers and New York City chapters of Romance Writers of America. She lives in Brooklyn, NY.

Website: www.katemcmurray.com
Twitter: @katemcmwriter
Facebook: facebook.com/katemcmurraywriter

Sign up for Kate's newsletter:
http://www.katemcmurray.com/newsletter

Like what you've read? A review on your favorite review or retail site is always greatly appreciated!